RISING SEA

JAMES LAWRENCE

Copyright 2019 by James Lawrence
All rights reserved.

ISBN: 9781797768489

This book is dedicated to my wife and family. Without their support and assistance, it would not have been possible to complete this book.

ABOUT THE AUTHOR

James Lawrence has been a soldier, small business owner, military advisor, and defense trader. He currently lives in the Middle East. He is the author of five novels in the Pat Walsh series; Arabian Deception, Arabian Vengeance, Arabian Fury, Arabian Collusion, and Rising Sea.

CHAPTER 1

SOUTH CHINA SEA, 1809

L ADY CHANG (CHING Shih before her marriage) held tightly to the door handle on the heavy wooden wardrobe to steady her balance. Once or twice a minute, a brilliant flash of lightning illuminated the dark, cramped stateroom through the pane glass window. The floor beneath her was in constant motion as the sixty-six-foot junk pitched and canted while crabbing its way ahead through the raging sea. This typhoon worried her more than any she'd ever encountered in her eight years of living at sea. The decision to sail into the storm was a gamble, but the stakes were high and she had no other option. Despite the situation, she remained resolute. Lady Chang was the leader of the largest pirate force in the world and she didn't earn command of a fleet of seventeen hundred junks and seventy thousand pirates by running away from danger.

The loud staccato beat of the heavy rain pelting against her stateroom window was interrupted by a booming thunderclap. The force of the thunder shook the window panes. Lady Chang wrapped herself in an oilskin, pushed the door open against the wind, and stepped out onto the poop-deck balcony to face the elements. From her perch on the balcony rail, she spotted the junk's captain below on the main deck. He had both hands on the wheel, his shoulders and head were down, and his feet were planted wide for balance. The captain of the *Key-ying* had a rope tied around his waist as an extra precaution. The scant storm rigging on the three masks held only a hint of canvas, but it was enough to give the experienced mariner all the control he needed to keep the nimble junk from being swamped.

The tumultuous weather matched her mood perfectly. Lady Chang's reign as leader of the Red Flags was coming to an end. The majority of the Red Flag junks were under the command of her husband, Chang Pao. His situation was even more desperate than her own. Chang Pao's fleet was trapped in the delta of the Pearl River by a combined force of Emperor Jiaqing's Navy and a Portuguese Fleet. It was because of the situation in the Pearl River Delta that she now found herself in this storm.

Chang Pao was a courageous leader and a brilliant tactician; her late husband had adopted the boy at an early age after recognizing his potential. Following the untimely death of her fifty-three-year old husband, she and her stepson married in order to retain control of the Red Flags. Lady Chang and her first husband had built the world's greatest pirate empire and she refused to allow the death of her husband and partner to destroy it.

The Red Flags were a tiny pirate force before the leader Cheng I rescued the demure prostitute Ching Shih out of a floating brothel in Canton. Many believed it was the clever Ching Shih who planted the idea of marriage in Cheng I's head. Others believed Cheng kidnapped her after recognizing her value as a strategist. Regardless of the reason, the decision altered Cheng's fortunes immensely. Cheng's brutality and Ching Shih's cunning combined to create the most powerful pirate fleet in the history of the world. Within a few short years, the Red Flags created a monopoly on pirating in South East China. Perhaps the biggest reason for the success was Ching Shih's unique management system. Many pirate captains willingly served under the Red Flag banner because of the certain prosperity and security that followed. In situations where gold and safety were insufficient motivation, it was not uncommon for pirate captains to be forced to pledge fealty to the Red Flag banner by sheer force. Ching Shih's pretty face, small stature, and gentle personality masked an iron will and a razor-sharp mind without equal in the South China Sea.

In Lady Chang's time, ownership did not pass to a wife upon the death of her husband. This was especially true in the pirating community. When Cheng I died, his widow had very little time to seduce her stepson—who was only a few years younger than herself— and shore up control of the Red Flags with a new union. The marriage between Cheng I's widow and her stepson was driven both by necessity and the heart. The union proved to be every bit as successful an alliance as her first marriage.

At their peak, the Red Flags controlled all of the coastal villages around Macau and Hong Kong. The villages had little option but to pay tribute to the strongest force in the region. Tributes from territorial possessions and bounties from seized merchant ships provided a reliable and lucrative income. Good things don't last forever; the death knell for the Red Flags came when the Qing Dynasty reversed a centuries-old policy and opened up the hermit kingdom for trade with Europe.

The control the Red Flags held over the trade routes into China was quickly recognized as a major impediment to commerce by the European powers. At the Europeans' prompting, the Emperor issued a proclamation directing the villages to cease paying tribute to the Red Flags. Forces were deployed to the coastal region to enforce the new proclamation. In retaliation for the Emperor's attempt to reclaim some of his own kingdom, Chang Pao launched a punitive strike deep into the Pearl River. He sacked, pillaged, and burned every village that failed to render a tribute payment. His attack reached all the way to the major city of Guangzhou. The attack was designed to serve as a warning to prevent future encroachments by the Emperor into Red Flag territory. At any other time, the brazen Chang Pao would have returned home victorious. What he didn't know this time was that the Portuguese government had deployed a fleet to help the Emperor deal with his pirate problem.

As Chang Pao withdrew from the Pearl River and entered the delta, he found his exit blocked at the narrowest point of the strait in a spot the locals referred to as the Tiger's Mouth. In the seventeen-mile-wide choke point between Macau and Hong Kong, he was confronted by six hundred of the Emperor's junks and six Portuguese warships. Fighting off his natural inclination to be aggressive, Chang Pao engaged the Portuguese in a series of probing actions over a week-long period. He tirelessly searched for a weakness to exploit in the Emperor's defenses, but he found none. Although Chang Pao's junks outnumbered the Chinese and Portuguese ships, the firepower advantage belonged to the Emperor. Each of the Portuguese warships had one hundred cannons while the average Red Flag junk could muster only fourteen. The defenders were anchored and would be able to fire many cannons from their broadsides into the attacking forces, while Chang Pao's advancing junks would find it much harder to bring their firepower to bear in a fight. It would have been suicide for Chang Pao to attack and foolish for the Emperor's forces to relinquish their defensive advantage and close with the Red Flags. Consequently, the two forces faced off against each other in a lasting stalemate, engaging in only minor skirmishes.

Upon learning of the entrapment and standoff, Lady Chang immediately traveled to the home of General Li Ch'ang-keng, the Chinese Regional Commander. She brought with her an escort of pirate wives and children. Lady Chang hoped the presence of the families might give her an advantage by humanizing the pirates who had been terrorizing the region for more than a decade. The uninvited visit caught the General by surprise. Lady Chang explained to the General that a battle would be very costly for both sides. She cautioned the General not to accept the huge cost in sailors and material required to destroy the Red Flag Pirate Fleet; she offered a much better resolution to the conflict. The General agreed to a negotiated settlement to the hostilities. When the terms were finalized, Lady Chang left her husband and his forces behind the cordon and embarked on a trip down the South China Sea to Palawan Island. She set out in a minor flotilla to retrieve from a hidden treasure cache the gold she needed to complete the financial terms of her agreement with the Chinese Government.

The journey from Macau to Palawan, Philippines, took two weeks. It was typhoon season, and travel across the South China Sea was perilous. On the return trip, Lady Chang's junk and two others from her twenty-ship armada were heavily laden with gold. Pirates don't have banks; they have hiding places. Lady Chang and her husband had two secret holes where they stored plunder. The secret hole in Macau was out of reach because it was on the wrong side of the Emperor's barricade. The second hiding spot was in a cave on the southern tip of Palawan Island.

Lady Chang descended the stairs and walked to the helm. Her hair instantly became matted by the heavy rain and the spray from the waves crashing against the hull. She joined Captain Chi under the small wooden roof that protected the helm station from the rain and sun.

"What news do you have?" Lady Chang asked her most trusted officer.

"The conditions are ripe for cyclones," Chi answered.

Lady Chang surveyed the sea around the junk. The rain made it difficult to see more than a thousand yards. When the sky lit up from a lightning bolt, she counted seven other vessels including the two that were carrying the treasure. The rest of the armada was beyond her sight.

"We need to seek safe harbor," Chi said.

She had only one month to fulfill her part of the agreement with the Emperor and the trip to Palawan had already consumed two weeks.

"Press on," Lady Chang ordered.

It was a good deal and she couldn't afford to default on it. She would pay the Emperor 130 thousand taels of gold and surrender her fleet to the government. In exchange, all of her men would be amnestied and her husband would receive a commission from the Emperor. Although the details of the agreement had not yet been shared with her men, she was certain they would be supportive of her decision. A big reason why she had been so successful as a pirate was not only due to the severity of her discipline but also because of her humanity. Tacked up on a board on the mast in front of her was a set of rules she posted on every ship:

- Lady Chang okays all attacks beforehand. Disobey, and you're beheaded.
- You give all loot to your superior, who distributes it afterward. Disobey once, you're beaten. Disobey twice, you're dead.
- Don't desert your post or take shore leave without permission. Disobey once, we cut off your ears (since you clearly weren't using them.) Disobey twice, you're dead.
- Rape a female captive, better believe that's a beheading.
- Have consensual sex with a female captive without permission, you're headless and she's taking a swim with a lead weight.
- If you want to have sex with a female prisoner, you take her as your wife. You are faithful to her. You treat her well. Or we take your head.
- Oh, and don't use the word "plunder." Instead, say "transferring shipment of goods." It just sounds nicer.

Lady Chang stood with Captain Chi against the driving rain. The dry comfort of her stateroom was only steps behind her, but she wanted to set an example for the crew of thirty-two onboard the *Key-ying*. Later in the afternoon, the sky began to lighten, and the intensity of the rain let up. For the first time in two days, she was able to see the sails of all twenty junks.

"Look," Captain Chi said, pointing to a funnel cloud forming over the dark sea.

"It's a cyclone," she replied.

The Captain turned the junk hard to port and the rest of the armada did the same. The ship increased sail and listed heavily to the starboard side as the junk ran almost perpendicular to the wind. The sea was rough, and the waves broke against the starboard side, spraying torrents of water across the deck. The armada raced to get out of the path of the cyclone as the funnel cloud bore down on the fleeing junks. The seamanship of Captain Chi and the crew was second to none. Even though they were riding low in the water with a heavy cargo, they managed to sprint ahead of the other junks in the armada. The formation became a strung-out column of fleeing junks. The armada was spread over a length of two miles when the ominous black funnel cloud overtook the line of escaping junks.

At the front of the column, Lady Chang and the *Key-ying* were engulfed in darkness. The Captain screamed for the sails to be furled and a heavy wind swept over the junk. Lady Chang and Captain Chi tied themselves to the wheel mount with a single line of rope as the pirates all around secured themselves as best they could. A giant wave forced the junk to a near vertical position before dropping it thirty feet backward into the sea.

When the junk slammed into the sea, the rear mast

snapped in half and a dozen pirates were swept off the stern deck and into the sea. The fury lasted less than half an hour until finally the sky brightened and the heavy seas returned to a more manageable state.

"Turn back and check for survivors," Lady Chang ordered.

"Aye," the captain replied.

Lady Chang surveyed the surrounding sea to locate the surviving junks. She searched mostly for the *Red Dragon* and the *Galloping Horse*, the two other junks carrying treasure. It was not until the next morning that a full accounting from the cyclone was made. The armada lost seven of its twenty junks and 247 personnel including pirates and family members. The biggest loss was the *Red Dragon*, which was carrying a third of the treasure. Knowing the perils of sea travel, Lady Chang had been wise to withdraw extra booty as a contingency should she lose a ship. She had all she needed in the holds of the *Key-ying* and the *Galloping Horse* to free her husband and conclude the deal.

CHAPTER 2

BAB AL MANDAB
STRAIT, RED SEA

CAPTAIN SONG STOOD behind the two-man console on the bridge of the Wuhu, a Type-054A guided missile frigate. The two junior officers seated in front of him at the helm stations were busy talking into the microphones attached to their headsets and adjusting the computer displays in front of them. The bridge officers managed the propulsion, navigation system, and deck operations of the one-hundred-and-thirty-meter stealth ship as it made its way south on the Red Sea toward the Gulf of Aden.

Song made sure Lieutenants Liu and Chin, his two bridge officers, were fully briefed before he stepped back from the bridge and entered the darkness of the Combat Information Center (CIC). The CIC was the nerve center of the frigate. It had an ultra-modern Star Wars ambience about it, with its vast array of computers, controls, and display screens. Operations within the CIC were grouped according to their respective combat roles and functions. The computer operators were grouped in clusters and each cluster was managed by a warfare officer.

As he made his rounds, Song checked that each man was fully engaged in his respective responsibilities. He gauged the professionalism of his officers as they each oversaw a cluster of system specialists. Every system specialist had his own console to operate and they each controlled an assigned sensor or weapon. He walked behind each of the working men and checked that their systems were operational and current.

In the back of the CIC, in an elevated chair overlooking the clusters, was his executive officer (XO). The XO was serving as the principal warfare officer of the entire center. The display in front of the XO displayed the ship's Combat Management System (CMS), which is an automated tactical command and control system that has a built-in Decision Support System (DSS). The CMS makes it possible to create situational awareness of everything going on inside and outside of the ship. One of the most critical functions of the CMS is that it builds a tactical picture that allows for the identification of threats, the evaluation of threats, and provides target assignments to weapon systems in situations where the threats must be destroyed. Operations in the CIC are networked together by an elaborate local area network that enables speedy and accurate information exchange within the CIC and enhances battlespace awareness and a rapid response to air, surface, and sub-surface threats. The tiny room was the brain of the frigate and the Wuhu had the most advanced brain in the entire Chinese Navy, a thought that filled Song with immense pride.

Song continued his walk clockwise around the room.

He stopped at each of the twelve workstations to check on the performance of his men. Satisfied that his frigate was operating properly as it escorted its convoy of two Saudi supertankers, he nodded to Commander Fang, his executive officer, and stepped outside and lit a cigarette. The morning November air in the Red Sea was crisp and cool—nothing like the balmy humid weather he had experienced when the tanker escort task force had first arrived on patrol in the region. The task force consisted only of three ships—two frigates and an oiler. He stood on a balcony that traversed the sides and rear of the bridge deck. From his position, he had almost a 360-degree view of the ship. He looked down at the rows of missile blast doors on the main deck and then farther up toward the bow until he found the 76mm Cannon. To the east, he had a clear view of the rocky brown coast of Eretria. The distant landmass to the west was the hills of Yemen. The reason he chose this moment to inspect the bridge and CIC was because the ship was at a heightened state of readiness. In only a few miles, the ship would enter the tightest part of the strait, where the shipping channel was only two miles wide and the distance between the coasts of Yemen and Eritrea were less than thirty miles apart.

Two Saudi oil tankers had been attacked and badly damaged by Houthi missiles only six months earlier. The Bab Al Mandab Strait was the most dangerous waterway in the world. Protecting the Chinese oil supply was the reason a rotating Chinese Naval Task Force routinely escorted Saudi oil through the dangerous strait. Captain Song lit a second cigarette and scanned forward with a pair of binoculars. It took a few moments, but he was able to locate the two black eleven-meter unmanned surface vehicles (USVs) bobbing in the water a mile to his front. The USVs were mine detectors. Each had a sonar system designed to find subsurface mines and alert the convoy prior to exposing the frigate to danger.

Content with the situation, he stubbed his cigarette out against the railing and re-entered the CIC. Song took his seat at the con in the center of the CIC. He put on his headset and leaned back in his comfortable captain's chair. Displayed on the wall in front of him was a large radar screen depicting the location of the convoy overlaying a naval chart. Two parallel icons of the USVs leading the convoy south through the narrow strait showed as blue diamonds. North of his position, he could see the black circular icons representing the two Liberian registered supertankers filled with Saudi oil. The supertankers were trailing his frigate which was represented in the center of the screen as a solid blue circle. Closer to the Yemeni coast, the radar displayed a picket line of Saudi and UAE patrol boats that made up the allied blockade designed to prevent supplies from reaching Houthi forces in Yemen.

"Two unidentified surface vectors approaching from the east," he heard his first officer say over the headset.

"Issue a verbal warning to change course," Song instructed.

"Make that six unidentified surface vectors approaching from the east. Range, six kilometers, speed thirty knots."

"Engage with the cannon if they get within two thousand meters," Song ordered.

"Two missile tracks inbound!" The targeting officer's alarmed voice shouted into his headset.

"Fire missiles; engage countermeasures," Song ordered in a calm, steady voice.

Four HQ-16 missiles burst from the front deck and, at supersonic speed, raced to intercept the Houthi-launched cruise missiles. The 76mm cannon began to rapid fire, pumping out a round every five seconds. Moments later the whirring burp of the AK-630 30mm rotary cannon filled the CIC.

"Missiles destroyed," the Weapons Officer reported.

"The trail tanker has been hit," the First Officer Reported.

"What hit the tanker?" the Captain asked.

"Two more missiles inbound," the First Officer interrupted.

"Fire missiles," ordered the Captain.

Four more HQ-16 missiles exploded from the honeycomb blast doors on the front deck.

An explosion shook the ship. The aluminum and composite hull was instantly breached midship. A second explosion went off in the stern and the ship began to fill with smoke. The ship instantly began to list to port and the lights flickered inside the CIC.

"Missiles destroyed, two more missiles inbound, firing," said the weapons officer in a panicked voice.

Four more HQ-16 shot into the sky from the badly damaged frigate. Unlike the previous missiles that after launch quickly turned into a flatter, more horizontal trajectory to intercept the low flying cruise missiles, these medium-range surface-to-air missiles continued straight up. The missiles were locked onto the radar signature of a much larger and higher target. The missiles sped high into the sky in pursuit of a pair of American F-18 Super Hornets that had been observing the action from what they thought was a safe altitude and distance. The Super Hornets were twenty-five thousand feet above the wounded frigate and ten miles South.

As soon as the radar from the frigate locked onto the Super Hornets, they took immediate evasive action. When they received the launch warning of a SAM missile in the air, the two Navy fighter jets triggered their countermeasures. The first HQ-16 detonated on a decoy. The second missile's semi-active radar homing seeker found a firm lock on the trail F-18 and, despite the best efforts of the pilot, the 70-kilogram warhead exploded within feet of the jet fighter and turned it into a fireball, instantly killing both crew members. The remaining two missiles fell harmlessly into the sea when they failed to acquire a target.

The surviving Super Hornet retaliated with an AMRAAM missile. The anti-ship missile followed the radar signature guiding the HQ-16 missiles. The AMRAAM hit the damaged Frigate directly in the center of the bridge, instantly killing the captain and all of the personnel inside the CIC and bridge. The Chinese frigate was fully engulfed in flames as it slowly sank to the bottom of the Red Sea.

The second Chinese frigate from the same Task Force was monitoring the situation one hundred nautical miles to the southeast in the Gulf of Aden. It tracked the surviving American Super Hornet on its return to the Aircraft Carrier, USS Harry Truman. As soon as the Super Hornet got within range of its HQ-16 air defense missiles, the Chinese frigate launched a volley of four missiles. The action took place more than one hundred miles from the Truman but was well within the protective umbrella of the Carrier Strike

Group. The air crew of the F-18 Super Hornet parachuted to safety after it was badly damaged by fragments from an exploding HQ-16. Before the two pilots ever hit the water, the Chinese frigate that launched the attack was simultaneously engaged and destroyed by a guided-missile destroyer and a Super Hornet flying close air patrol above the Carrier Strike Group.

CHAPTER 3

ELEUTHERA, BAHAMAS

I WAS AT MY desk doing paperwork when my cell rang. It was Mike, so I answered.

"I'm on final approach to Governors Harbour. Can you pick me up?"

"Sure, be there in ten," I said, grateful to put some distance between me and my upcoming tax bill.

I went downstairs and walked out the front door. I looked down at the driveway from the front stairs and noticed my Tahoe was missing; Cheryl must have taken it into town. I went back in and found the keys to her Carrera. I had to practically fold myself to get my 6'5" frame into the tiny silver sports car. Fortunately, the Governors Harbour Airport is only a short drive north from my beach house.

I found Mike standing outside the small white terminal building and pulled up in front of him.

"What's this, a mid-life crisis?" he asked.

"Cheryl took my truck; just be glad you don't have to fit any luggage into this thing."

"At least it's a convertible; otherwise you'd have to stick your head through the sunroof and drive it like a clown car."

"It's better than walking. Are you hungry or do you want to get straight down to business?"

"Business, but let's wait until we get to your office."

"Fine," I said.

"When's the last time you did a sweep of your office?"

"A couple of days ago."

"That'll have to be good enough."

I turned left off Banks Road and onto the white brick driveway of my house. I pressed the gate opener and the black wrought iron gates parted, allowing me to drive the remaining five hundred yards to the garage. I parked the car inside the garage and led Mike up the back stairs to my office on the third floor. Mike waited until Maria, the housekeeper, served us coffee before getting down to the purpose of his visit. My office takes up the entire third floor and it has a great view because it's high enough to see the Caribbean and the Atlantic over the trees if you look west and east respectively. We moved to the seating area next to the picture window overlooking the Atlantic. I was on the couch and Mike was in the lounger, catty-corner to me. He leaned forward and placed a laptop on the coffee table and then turned it on and unlocked it. He faced the laptop, so we could both see the screen, and then he leaned back in the heavy recliner.

"What do you know about the incident with the Chinese off the coast of Yemen?" he asked.

"Just what's in the papers. Last week the Houthis attacked a Saudi tanker convoy escorted by a Chinese frigate in the BAM strait. One of the Saudi oil tankers was badly damaged, and a Chinese frigate was sunk."

"All of that's true, but there's more to the story. We had two Super Hornets on patrol above the action. They were from the Truman Carrier Strike Group that was a couple of days from finishing up a deployment to the region. After it was hit and badly damaged by the Houthis, the Chinese guided missile frigate locked on and engaged both of our fighters. We don't know why they targeted our fighters when they were under attack by a Houthi surface threat. Anyway, we lost one fighter in the initial missile salvo. A second Super Hornet was able to evade the missile attack and then delivered the fatal shot to the frigate."

"Tensions are already very high between the US and China over trade; I can't imagine how the Chinese reacted to us sinking a frigate."

"Badly, they reacted very badly, and it gets worse. The Chinese maintain a permanent escort task force in the Gulf of Aden. They keep two guided missile frigates and an oiler on station to keep the waterway open to protect their energy supply. While the first frigate was escorting the oil tankers from the Red Sea through the BAM straight to the Gulf of Aden, the second Chinese frigate was positioned southeast in the Gulf of Aden. The second Chinese frigate followed the action and then shot down the surviving Super Hornet as it was returning to the Truman. At that point, the Truman Carrier Strike Group intervened and sank the Chinese frigate. Two of the Super Hornet pilots survived and two were killed. The Chinese lost two of their most modern frigates along with more than two hundred and fifty sailors."

"I can't believe none of this has been in the news."

"Some of it's already out, the rest is about to be. Initially, both sides tried to keep a lid on it. The Chinese to save face, the US, to buy some time while we sought out a way to ease the tensions."

"What's changed?"

"The Chinese have escalated. Yesterday, they shot down two of our reconnaissance planes over the South China Sea. The American death toll is now at thirteen."

"What's going to happen next?"

"Before any of these incidents occurred, the Lincoln Carrier Strike Group set off on a deployment to the South China Sea to conduct a freedom of navigation (FON) exercise. The Lincoln is still in the middle of the Pacific, but the Chinese have made it clear that if the Lincoln enters their territorial waters in the South China Sea, they'll sink it."

"The FON is going into the disputed areas?"

"Almost all of the South China Sea is a disputed area. The Chinese territorial claim is outrageous. The nine-mile boundary the Chinese claim as their waters has already been ruled against by the UN. The Chinese claim is basically the entire SCS minus the 12-mile territorial waters of the other countries."

"It's hard to believe the Chinese could sink an American Carrier Group. Last I checked, they only had one aircraft carrier and that one had a ski lift runway because they can't figure out how to build a catapult."

"It's not that they can't figure out how to build a catapult—I'm sure they stole those designs years ago. It has to do with the engine power on their jets."

"Why is the US afraid of a Navy with only one half-assed aircraft carrier?"

"They may only have one carrier that holds less than a third of the aircraft that a US carrier does and takes forever to launch and recover. But what they do have is three fixed aircraft carriers with three-thousand-meter runways that more than do the job."

"What's a fixed aircraft carrier?"

"The Chinese have constructed naval bases with airfields on the reef islands. Three of the islands—Fiery Cross, Subi, and Mischief—have airfields with more than fifty fighter jets apiece. The remaining four bases service surface ships, unmanned surface vehicles, and submarines. All are fortified and have robust air defenses. The Chinese forces arrayed in the SCS could easily swarm and defeat a US Carrier Strike Group."

"Why is the Lincoln going into the SCS then?"

"The FON was planned before the escalation in hostilities. If the US fails to follow through, it would be very bad. Once we back down to China, every partner we have in Asia will know we're no longer with them. Taiwan, Japan, Korea, the Philippines; we can't abandon our obligations."

"The plan is to start World War III instead?"

"That's the rub; we don't want to do that either. Which brings me to why I'm here."

"I don't do diplomacy. I thought you knew that."

"I do know that. I have a mission for you that is much more within your skill set," Mike said as he reached over and opened a file on the laptop.

"What am I looking at?"

"This is Operation Zhang Ha—that's Chinese for Rising Sea, which is what the Chinese call the South China Sea."

"What's on the video file?"

"It's a computer simulation of a man-made tsunami. Those South China Sea bases that are giving us so much trouble are only a few feet above sea level. You're going to unleash a thirty-foot wave that's going to sweep the jets and the air defenses off the three island airbases and turn them back into sand bars."

"How does exploding a nuclear bomb underwater not start World War III?"

"It won't take a nuke. It can be done with conventional explosives and it won't be detectable as an explosion because the explosion is going to be drowned out by the earthquake you're going to set off. Just watch the simulation," Mike said, as he hit the play icon.

The video showed a map of the South China Sea. The simulation highlighted Palawan Island, the Philippines, and then west of the island it showed a fault line under the sea. The fault was labeled Wa-Nu and it identified it as a strike-slip fault line. Next, the simulation showed the positioning of explosives across a ten-mile section of the fault. The explosives were placed past the edge of the continental shelf where the water becomes very deep in an area called the Palawan Trench. The cartoon-like simulation showed the explosives detonating and then depicted a section of the shelf falling into the Palawan Trench. A small ripple appeared on the surface of the sea. The ripple moved west toward a cluster of man-made islands; the two highlighted were Fiery Cross Reef and Hughes Reef. The wave traveled hundreds of miles and then the simulation showed a side shot as the wave neared the islands, grew to a height of thirty feet, and crashed over the islands. The wave was followed by two more, smaller waves with the same effect.

"What about the damage to civilians?" I asked.

"It's going to take over an hour for the wave to reach the target. Tsunami warnings will be issued and, in the few occupied islands in the area, the people will get to high ground and the US will assist them to rebuild. The reef islands will be completely destroyed. The Chinese will have time to prepare; they may even launch their aircraft and ships and that's fine. All we care about is that after the wave hits, they won't have any usable airfields."

"And the villain will be a natural disaster and not the USA."

"Exactly."

We spent the rest of the afternoon going over the logistics and the technical details of the explosive emplacement and detonation. I took Mike back to his waiting jet and made it back home before Cheryl arrived. She found me up in my office.

"What are you doing?" she asked.

"I just booked a flight for both of us to Paphos."

"Why, what's up?"

"Mike came this afternoon. We have a new mission."

"Doing what?" she asked.

"We're going to start an earthquake that will create a tsunami and wipe out the Chinese Naval Bases in the South China Sea."

"Is that all?"

"Yeah, we need to leave first thing tomorrow morning. I'm putting in some gear requests to the guys in Cyprus, so they can be ready when we arrive. Mike already sent the mission-critical equipment."

"What about the innocent people? Is this tsunami going to kill innocent people?"

"According to Mike, the South China Sea tsunami early warning system will kick in and nobody will get hurt."

"How are you getting to the South China Sea? Are you going to take the boat?"

"Yeah, we're going to take the *Sam Houston*. We're going to false flag the yacht as a treasure hunter from Singapore."

"Am I coming?"

"Of course, we'll take the whole team."

"How long is this going to take?"

"We'll be operating between the Spratly Islands and Palawan Island, right in the middle of the disputed boundary between China and the Philippines. It's a little over twenty-five hundred nautical miles from Cyprus. That's going to take a week and a half, depending on how long we have to wait to get through the Suez."

"It sounds like you have this all figured out."

"Not me. Mike must have had an entire team working on this day and night. He's got everything planned down to the tiniest detail."

CHAPTER 4

PAPHOS, CYPRUS

C HERYL AND I landed in Paphos International and went directly to the Trident Hangar on the cargo side of the airport. It was a mild, sunny winter day, and because we couldn't find a taxi, we decided to roll our bags the half a mile around the airport perimeter fence to the Trident Hangar entrance.

"I'm glad I didn't wear heels," Cheryl said.

"We're operational. Nothing but combat boots from now on."

"Does Ferragamo make combat boots?"

"This is going to be your first time out with the team on an operation. You're going to find that when I'm in the role as captain of a fighting ship, I'm a different man, not the easy-going guy you know and love. I run a tight ship. I'm not sure if you can handle the discipline of being on a ship of war with me."

"Your ship of war has a better wine cellar than the Queen Elizabeth II."

"We don't sacrifice our comforts, but that doesn't mean

I won't have you keelhauled if I get any of that backtalk you're so famous for." Cheryl just smiled.

"You don't scare me, Captain."

We entered the hangar from the side door. Once inside the cavernous metal hangar, we found the team sorting and inspecting equipment inside a fenced-off area on the far side.

Migos was driving a forklift with a sea sled, a STIDD DPD, balanced on the front of the tines. When he saw us, he stopped the forklift and got off to meet us. The rest of the team noticed us and began to amble over. McDonald was next, followed by Savage and Sorenson. The seven of us are an eclectic team. Migos is a former special forces operator, his Greek heritage evident in his face and heavily muscled Mediterranean physique. McDonald is a retired Navy special warfare medic with years of experience with the DEVGRU, the SEAL Teams, and SWCC. McDonald is my second-in-command. He's a Midwesterner with quiet mannerisms and the countenance of a small-town gentleman. Savage and Sorenson are both new to the team. Both came out of the Combat Actions Group in Fort Bragg, my old Army unit. Savage is from Hawaii; he's biracial, a mix of Pacific Islander and African American. Savage is about six feet with the lean hard features of an NFL defensive end. Sorenson is from Wisconsin and looks like the Viking King in the kids' cartoon *How to Train Your Dragon*; Sorenson's nickname is Shrek. The rest of them just go by their last names.

We spent the rest of the day provisioning and loading the boat. I keep the *Sam Houston* in the Paphos Marina, which is just a few miles from the airport. The boat, an Azimut 64 motor yacht, was going to be cramped with all six of us aboard. The Azimut is a very high-end luxury yacht made in Italy— a performance yacht built to handle the toughest seas. It's a comfortable ride with three well-appointed staterooms in the lower deck, a salon, galley, and wheelhouse in the main deck, and a helm station and lounge area on the top deck. Migos and McDonald would share a stateroom as would Sorenson and Savage. Cheryl and I would be in the owner's cabin at the bow. The yacht originally came with two additional bunks in the crew quarters, but I converted that space to fuel storage. Eliminating the crew quarters allowed me to extend the range of the yacht to over two thousand nautical miles.

Most of the stern deck and the hydraulic ramp perched on the back were packed with equipment. We had racks of gas cylinders filled with air and normoxic tri-mix for the deep dives. We had two underwater sleds, an underwater scooter, a Seabotix ROV and a Gavia AUV. A thirteen-foot RIB tender was lashed to the hydraulic ramp. Across from the racks of cylinders were our diving rigs, dry suits, and the buoyancy kits needed for salvage. With all of the gear, there was very little room to move on the stern deck.

We were underway by mid-morning the day after we arrived in Paphos. What took the most time was stocking the galley with food. Cheryl took over the culinary side of the operation and she had very strong ideas on what was needed. I decided not to quibble about a few lost hours.

The late fall weather was mild as we made our way south and east through the Suez and the Red Sea. We only had to wait two days to enter the canal thanks to a generous donation I made to the Egyptian harbormaster's retirement fund. The narrow strait between Yemen and the Horn of

Africa has always been a challenge because of pirates, but now with Houthi, Iranian, Saudi, and Emirati forces all facing off in the waters, the path was even more daunting. We ran day and night at a cruising speed of twenty-four knots until we reached the open waters in the Gulf of Aden.

We crossed the Arabian Sea and refueled in Colombo, Sri Lanka. From Colombo, we headed due east and then passed through the crowded Malacca Strait between Malaysia and Indonesia to the South China Sea. Once we reached the South China Sea, it was a five-hundred-mile straight shot northeast until we reached Sabah, Malaysia. We made the trip in eight days operating day and night. McDonald and I took turns at the helm while the rest of the team readied the equipment.

We refueled at the Sutera Harbour Marina in Sabah. I gave the crew a night of shore leave and stayed on the boat with Cheryl. It's a crowded marina and we didn't draw too much attention. Cheryl brought in a cleaning crew and we changed out the linens and refilled the water tanks. I went to the marina grocery store and bought some fresh groceries. When I returned, it was late afternoon and the cleaning crew was gone, I found Cheryl in the salon watching a movie.

"When are you going to brief the guys?" she asked.

"Tomorrow morning, once we get underway."

"Any updates from Mike?"

"Everything's a go. The payload will be dropped today; everything is on schedule."

"What are we going to do tonight?"

"I'd like to go to dinner and get a room at the Shangri La down the street. But we can't afford to leave the boat unattended. If a piece of equipment walked away, we'd be in serious trouble. Better to stay on the boat."

"I'll have something delivered to the boat. You can find a bottle of wine. I'll make you happy you stayed on the boat with me," she said with a smile.

"It's nice to be alone."

"No kidding. The boat's never been so crowded."

The next morning everybody was back on board by seven and we set sail for Antelope Shoal which is located about twelve miles west of Quezon, Palawan. The trip was five hours at cruising speed. At lunch, McDonald was at the controls in the wheelhouse and the other three guys were seated in the galley directly behind. Cheryl was serving hamburgers.

"Up until now, I wasn't authorized to disclose the mission. Now that we're on the last leg, I can fill you in on the purpose of this trip. I gave the team a detailed rundown of the backstory with the US Navy and the Chinese in the Gulf of Aden and later in the South China Sea. I told them about the upcoming deployment and timing. None of the guys had any questions about the why; they were only concerned about the how, what, and when. I gave a detailed timeline and operations order. I provided written instructions for each person and the tasks they had to perform. After lunch, Cheryl took the wheel and I showed the simulation of the tsunami to the team on the big screen TV in the salon.

"How much damage is the tsunami going to create?" asked Migos, who was sitting on one of the pale leather couches.

"The wave, when it reaches land, is going to be over thirty feet. The reef islands are only a few feet above sea level. The wave is going to pass completely over each of the islands and destroy the runway, the planes, the hangars, and the buildings. There will be at least two smaller waves following behind the first that will do further damage."

"How far will the wave go? Will it reach Vietnam or China?"

"You saw the simulation. Yes, it will, but won't be near the force of what will hit the target islands. A tsunami warning will be issued and they'll have hours of warning. The damage isn't expected to be much."

"What about on the target islands? Will they get a tsunami warning?"

"They will; they'll have at least an hour of warning, which will give the people time to protect themselves and maybe allow some of the aircraft to get away."

"This is like Pearl Harbor. We're going to attack them without warning," said McDonald.

"We're going to give them warning. The UN has already ruled that China has violated the territorial rights of the Philippines, Vietnam, Brunei, and a bunch of other countries. We're going to end their violation of the sovereign territorial rights of those other countries and we're even going to give them an hour's warning. It seems likely there will be Chinese deaths, but they'll be kept to a minimum and unlike with Pearl Harbor, when it's over, if we do this right, the Chinese will believe it was caused by Mother Nature and it won't lead to a world war."

"Do you really believe that?" asked Migos.

"Yes, I do. The only thing I don't one hundred percent believe is how less than thirty thousand pounds of explosive is going to cause an earthquake."

"You're not totally sure this will work?"

"Neither is the CIA. Computer models are one thing, but we won't know for certain until we try it. Creating an earthquake and generating a tsunami of this size are two things that have never been done."

"Never?" asked Migos.

"In 1944 the US did some experiments with conventional explosives in New Zealand and found they could generate mini tsunamis, but nothing as big as what we're talking about here. They called it Operation Seal and it was very hush-hush at the time."

"So, this could work," said McDonald.

"If we do everything right—if we get the explosives to the right depth and the right coordinates and detonate everything simultaneously, we'll have done our job. Whether or not the science is going to work is well beyond my pay grade," I said.

CHAPTER 5

ANTELOPE SHOAL, SOUTH CHINA SEA

W E ANCHORED IN sixty feet of water above Antelope Shoal, which is a submerged sandy ridge located just to the west of Palawan Island. We were thirteen miles off the Philippines coast in the disputed area between China and the Philippines. It was dusk when we arrived, and the bright orange glow of the sun was touching the South China Sea on the western horizon. The sea was a little rough and Migos almost got tossed in when he was leaning over to place the yellow torpedo-shaped autonomous unmanned vehicle (AUV) into the warm ocean water.

The AUV was on a pre-set course to find our explosive cache and then provide detailed imagery of the detonation points, located in caves along a massive sea cliff only two hundred yards west from our anchor point. The sea cliff is the end of the continental shelf and it extends all the way down to the Palawan Trench, the third deepest spot in the world. The base of the cliff we were working on is six thousand feet deep. In one spot, known as the Galathea Depth, the Palawan Trench is 34,580 feet deep. We were going to place forty-two hundred pounds of HBX-1 explosives into five different shallow caves along that sea cliff. The depths of the caves ranged from 387 to 511 feet beneath the surface.

We recovered the four-and-a-half-foot-long AUV three hours later. It was easy to spot the white strobe light in the night sky once it breached the surface. I was already very confident we were over the explosive cache because the yacht's sonar was reflecting an image of a rectangular box with the same dimensions as a forty-foot container. The explosives had been delivered by a US Navy nuclear submarine earlier in the day.

I spent the next two hours with Cheryl and McDonald looking at what the AUV had found. The AUV was equipped with an obstacle avoidance sonar, a side scan sonar, a camera in the nose, and a magnetometer. I was mostly interested in the sonar mapping of the cliff. We'd been given coordinates by Mike for the placement of the explosive, but we needed to confirm them with the sonar images. Once confirmed, we uploaded the dive plans into the four dive computers and the two ARNAV navigation systems on the STIDD DPD sleds.

At the depths we were going to be working, every move had to be planned in detail—not just the depth, but the rate of ascent and descent as well as the duration of each stop. The dive computers on the Poseiden7 tech closed-circuit breathing systems, which can be used to a depth of six hundred feet, are state of the art. At the depths we were working, the most time one person could spend at a detonation point in a single day was forty-five minutes, which meant the four of us were going to have to make maximum use of our time. The job was going to take five days, which is why our cover story as treasure hunters was so important.

Migos, Sorenson, and Savage reviewed the footage on the laptop located on the galley table and then verified it against the data entered into their dive computers. The dive computer on a rebreather connects to the rig. The dive computer is the brain that determines gas flows and other critical operating functions beyond just navigation, depth, and decompression data.

I woke up early the next morning filled with nervous energy. Cheryl was still asleep when I went upstairs to make coffee. I found McDonald already awake sitting at the galley table reviewing the AUV data on the control unit's laptop.

"What are you doing?" I asked.

"Migos snores. It was better on the voyage out when I was on night shift and he was on day shift." I laughed.

"He snores terribly; sometimes he even talks in his sleep. He's a terrible roommate. I've spent more time with him than with Cheryl."

"Anyway, I came up here to get away from the man-sized Ken doll and decided to check our work last night. That's when I found this."

"What this?" I asked, as I slid in next to him on the bench next to the table.

"It's a magnetometer reading taken between demolition point three and demolition point four."

"Can you see anything on the camera or sonar?"

"No, but there's definitely something in that general area that has some heavy metal."

"When we get done today, we should launch the AUV

to have another look. Make it do a search pattern from above and zig zag it down the wall of the cliff."

"I'll do that."

"If nothing else, when the Philippine Navy or the Chi-Coms come by, we can show them that we really are searching for stuff, being treasure hunters and all."

Sorenson showed up a while later wearing his drysuit.

"Aren't you dying in that thing?" I asked.

"I am, I just wanted to make sure it fit over the thermals."

"Looks like it does. You may want to take it off before you stroke out on us."

"It's a good quality suit. How did you know my size?"

"I didn't. That came from the CIA; they know everything about you because of your former life with the boys."

After breakfast, Migos and I put our rigs on. The Poseiden7 looks like a black plastic backpack with two gas cylinders on each side. The mouthpiece is on a loop, and the air doesn't escape on a closed-circuit breathing system, but instead gets recycled. The system monitors the oxygen level in the loop and scrubs out the CO_2 and adds oxygen to maintain a consistent level of air, or in our case for this deep dive, trimix. The hydraulic ramp was crowded. The thirteen-foot tender that is usually perched on the ramp was already in the water, tied off to the stern tow mounting to make room for the two sleds that crowded the ramp. With the tender off the deck, there was at least enough room to move around. It was 85 degrees and I was sweating up a storm as I put on my fins and stepped into the water. Migos and I gave each other a thumbs up before releasing the air in our buoyancy compensator vests and slowly descending to the shoal sixty feet below.

Several minutes later we were swimming above the explosives. The top of the metal container was a green, black, and sand camouflage-patterned plastic tarp. We untied the tarp and folded it back. Inside the container box were thirty metal pods that each looked like a big aircraft bomb. The pods were stacked in ten rows and three columns. There was one box in the container that had pre-cut lines of detonation cord packed in five bags for each detonation site. I removed one bag and clipped it to my vest. Migos and I then positioned six pods outside the container on the sea floor in a row.

I watched as a STIDD sled glided into position next to the pods we had lined up. The second sled piloted by Sorenson parked next to it. Migos and I moved to the closest pod and attached it to the hitch on the back of the closest sled. Then we attached a second pod to the second sled. The pods were STIDD cargo pods filled with seven hundred pounds of explosives each. Under the water with the flotation foam in the pods, it was easy to manipulate them into position and attach them. Despite weighing seven hundred pounds each, they were neutrally buoyant and light as a feather.

I moved to the first sled and gave Savage a thumbs up. He got off the sled and I got on, lying head-first horizontally on my stomach. When I saw Migos was on his sled, I hit the go button on the ARNAV systems. The sleds have three settings; manual, autopilot, and autonomous. For this leg of the journey, the sled moved on autopilot based on the settings we inputted last night.

The water at sixty feet was blue and clear. I could see the hull of the *Sam Houston* above and beyond the golden rays of the sun. Moving at three knots, it took only a few minutes to reach the edge of the shelf. Suddenly, the sea floor disappeared and below me was absolute darkness. I monitored my dive computer to make sure the sled was descending at the prescribed rate. It took over five minutes to reach a depth of 478 feet. The headlight of the sled illuminated the wall of the sea cliff. I found the opening to the cave and verified the coordinates with the internal navigation system on the ARNAV. Migos pulled up beside me. I put the sled in manual mode and drove it into the mouth of the cave. Migos followed behind. Ten yards into the cave, I stopped the sled and landed it on the cave floor. I got off and detached the pod. Migos did the same. We backed the sleds out of the cave and switched them to autonomous mode. We sent the sleds back to Sorenson and Savage.

I guided the lead pod another fifty yards into the cave. Migos brought his pod next to mine and we connected the two with det-cord. The cave was big enough for both of us to swim next to each other, which was good because it was going to make it easy to turn around. It was completely dark in the cave except for the lights we had mounted on the top of our masks. We made the fifty-yard return trip to the mouth of the cave and waited for the sleds to arrive with another load of pods. Standing on the ledge, with our backs to the cave, we looked out into the dark water. Beneath us, it was ink black. Above, there was some light filtering down from the sun, but it was very dim and without the aid of a flashlight, many of the colors were filtered out. Our drysuits were red, but appeared black; fortunately, we had reflective tape on our arms that made finding each other easy.

I checked my dive computer and it indicated that we had to begin our ascent in eleven minutes. If the sleds didn't arrive in the next two minutes, we'd lose a full day, because we would have to dive this same location a second time. Migos tapped my shoulder and pointed. The headlight on the first sled came into view. We both swam out to intercept it as its twin props reversed to a stop in front of the cave. The second sled wasn't far behind. I left Migos and went to the second one. I detached the pod and sent the sled back to Sorenson and Savage. I was in a hurry, so I swam with the pod in front of me like a kickboard. Migos was in front of me doing the same. When we got to where we positioned the first two pods, we both checked our dive computers and signaled each other to turn back. I left a marker light on the bag with the det-cord and connected it to the pod closest to the cave entrance.

I followed Migos to the cave entrance. I wrapped the bungee cord of another Mark-Light around a rock and twisted the cap to turn it on. Migos and I were swimming next to each other staring at the computer screens attached to our right wrists that were guiding our rate of ascent. It got brighter as we went up. At three hundred feet we found the six large steel dive cylinders that made up our emergency gas supply. Migos and I stopped at the gas tanks that were attached to the end of the *Sam Houston's* anchor line. Once everyone was in the water, McDonald had repositioned the *Sam Houston* over the detonation point and dropped our bail-out tanks on the yacht's anchor. We both hung onto the anchor line and waited for the clocks on our dive computers to count down so we could move to the next decompression stop. Tied to the anchor line above the dangling cylinders was a mesh dive bag with plastic water bottles. I removed the regulator from my mouth and drank half a bottle.

For the next four hours and eighteen minutes, Migos and I moved up the anchor line from decompression stop to decompression stop. Below us, we could see Sorenson and Savage doing the same. When Sorenson and Savage were done connecting the last demolition pods, they sent the sleds to the surface and joined us on the anchor line. Monitoring the progress of both dive teams was a green, box-shaped Seabotix ROV with a single claw arm. The ROV was on a tether line to a control unit in the *Sam Houston*. The cameras and sonar sensors on the ROV kept watch on our condition and progress and served as an alarm system in case a safety diver was needed. As the hours passed, the dark hull of the yacht above got closer and closer. When we finally breached the surface, I inflated my buoyancy compensator fully and spat out the mouthpiece. I was exhausted, my jaw hurt from biting the mouthpiece, and it felt so good to breathe fresh air again. We both swam to the hydraulic ramp which was positioned three feet below the surface and we sat upright on the ledge of the ramp.

The ramp raised us out of the water. I disconnected and unhooked my rig and I felt it lifted off my shoulders from behind. I removed my fins and handed them and my mask back behind me. When I stood up, I was a little wobbly from fatigue. Cheryl took my arm and led me onto the deck. McDonald did the same with Migos.

"How did it go?"

"Everything worked perfectly," I said. Cheryl and McDonald laughed.

"What's so funny?" I asked.

"You sound like Donald Duck," Cheryl said.

"It's the helium; it will wear off in a bit."

I went downstairs to my stateroom to shower while Cheryl and McDonald stowed our equipment and prepared it for the next day's dive. When I returned, Sorenson and Savage were already on the deck.

The deck was getting crowded again with six of us, the two sleds, and the rest of the equipment. I found the hulking Sorenson sitting on the couch facing the bow.

"Did you connect all six pods?" I asked.

"Yeah, everything went great. We had time at the cache, so we set up the next six pods for movement."

"Awesome. Do you feel ok?"

"Yeah, I'm a little dehydrated and a lot hungry, that's all."

"It was a solid dive plan."

Migos came over and slapped Sorenson on the back.

"We need to take some video of Shrek talking in that squeaky helium voice," he said.

"Don't joke about recording anything on this mission. When we're done, we're going to erase every piece of data that shows we were ever here. Dive computers, navigation systems, everything—even your Fitbit if you have one," I said in a very serious voice. Migos stopped joking. He could tell this mission was going to keep me on edge until it was done.

I walked to the hydraulic ramp and helped McDonald lift the ROV out of the water. The underwater robot was connected to a six-hundred-meter thin tether line wrapped in a big spool on the starboard side of the stern. Several underwater writing pads were next to the spool in case the need arose to send a message down to the divers or vice versa.

I went to the kitchen and removed a pan of thick

rib-eye steaks. I balanced the pan with one arm while I carried them up the steep stairs to the flydeck. I turned on the gas grill and removed a Sam Adams Winter Ale from the fridge. A few minutes later, Migos and Cheryl joined me. Cheryl was carrying a salad and Migos had a basket of sourdough bread.

"The potatoes and corn will be ready in fifteen minutes," Cheryl said.

"We're all starving," I replied.

Savage, Sorenson, and McDonald finished installing fresh batteries in the sleds and preparing the equipment for the next day's dive. We all sat around the table after dinner and programmed our dive computers. McDonald and Cheryl had already calculated the data and McDonald programmed the sled ARNAVs. It was dark by the time we were finished. I moved the yacht back over to Antelope Shoal. Our demolition positions were all on the sea wall; the shallow water in Antelope Shoal was in the center of the line of demo positions. The route to the demo positions was longest on the first and last positions, shorter on the second and fourth, and shortest on the third. The routes to and from the demolition cache looked like a Chinese fan if diagrammed out. We were planning on our second day to complete the second demo position and finish half of the third.

After I dropped anchor, I found McDonald on the stern deck moving the yellow Gavia AUV onto the hydraulic lift.

"Are you going to finish that survey of the wall where you found the metal?" I asked.

"Yeah, I'm going to do a zig-zag pattern of the wall from the top of the shelf all the way down to one thousand meters."

"How long is that going to take?"

"Seven hours at three knots."

"That's a lot of data."

"It is. During your dive tomorrow, the data will transfer over the boat's LAN and I'm going to build a 3D map of that section of the wall."

"What for?" I asked.

"I'm curious about the metal return and I want to see what the AUV can do."

"Knock yourself out. I'm heading to bed; four hours of hanging onto the anchor line while decompressing wore me out."

I found Cheryl charging batteries in the engine room when I got below deck.

"I'm going to bed," I said.

"I need a few more minutes; I'll join you soon."

I don't know when Cheryl did join me, because I was out like a light. When I woke up the next morning it felt like deja-vu from the previous morning. I left Cheryl sleeping and found McDonald at the galley table working the AUV data on his laptop. The morning weather was great, the sky was sunny, and the sea was calm when Migos and I drove off the back ramp in a pair of STIDD sleds.

Many hours later, Migos and I were dangling off the anchor line that was positioned next to demolition site three when we heard a ship propeller above. Looking up, I could see the bottom of a hull move abreast of the *Sam Houston* on its port side. The hull was bigger than the *Sam Houston*; I estimated it at eighty to ninety feet. From our vantage point, that's all we could tell. The other ship remained abreast of the *Sam Houston* until we had only five minutes to go in our last decompression stop and then it departed.

"Who were our visitors?" I asked when Cheryl removed my rig.

"Philippine Navy. They asked what we were doing, checked our registration. Stared at you guys for a while on the ROV monitor and left."

"They bought the treasure hunter story."

"Yeah, they did."

"Good cover, then."

The next morning, I found McDonald at his normal position behind his laptop at the galley table. I poured myself a hot cup of coffee from the steel thermos coffee pot.

"Come and have a look at this," McDonald said. I walked over and slid in beside him.

"What am I looking at?"

"It's a shelf on the sea wall. It's about thirty feet wide."

"Yea, I can see that."

"Look at how the shelf bulges here," he said.

"It does that in a lot of places," I said.

"It does, but the shape of this bulge isn't natural. It's straight in the middle and it curves up in the front and the back."

"I can't see that; it has too much growing on it," I said.

"Let me zoom out." The side scan sonar image zoomed out and I saw what McDonald was talking about. It looked like a small ship was balanced on the shelf.

"The shape looks like a junk. Is this where the metal readings are coming from?"

"Yeah, lots of metal, especially for a wooden junk."

"Where is this location in relation to demo position four?" I asked.

McDonald zoomed out farther and showed a picture of a large section of the wall. He hit a key and all five demo positions showed against the dark background of the wall. He moved an arrow cursor on the screen to point.

"This is demo point four; it's at 518 feet. The shelf is at 284 feet and its 417 yards along the wall towards demo point three."

"Migos and I will be done at least ten minutes earlier today. Let's recalculate the dive and have us detour to the wreck on our way up after we're done with the demo."

"Just you and Migos?" he asked.

"Yes, just us. It's too late to reprogram the sleds. We'll have a look and then swim back to the *Sam Houston*."

"I think that's too dangerous. Why don't we check it out with the ROV when you guys are done today?"

"You're right. I'm too excited; this is my first treasure hunt. I can't wait to see what's in that ship."

"It's at 274 feet. Cheryl and I could dive it this afternoon when you guys are done after we've had a look at it with the ROV."

"That's a better idea. When we're down today, you should prep for the dive. We also need to get the bags and recovery gear ready."

When everyone was awake and in the galley, I asked McDonald to share his news. The high risk deep-water technical dives we were performing were physically and emotionally draining. The team was exhausted, and the energy level was very low. The idea of creating a tsunami wave and possibly endangering innocents was an added burden that weighed on us all. The news of finding a wreck and possibly a treasure was like a surge of electricity that lit the room up with excitement and picked up everyone's spirits.

"What's the plan, boss?" asked Migos.

"Well, I realize none of us are all that fired up about our current mission but completing the next three dives takes priority over everything else. Today after we're done, we'll use the ROV and poke around the wreck. If we find something, we'll send Cheryl and McDonald down to have a closer look."

"I'm on board with that," Cheryl said with a big grin.

"Today we finish demo positions three and four. Tomorrow is a long leg; we finish demo position five. The day after tomorrow the only two people who are scheduled to dive are Migos and me. We're going to use the sleds and emplace the limpet mines on all five sites. We'll change that. While Migos and I are arming the sites, you guys will be diving the wreck. We'll synch the mines to detonate the next day. That means we can dive on the wreck today and for three more days before we have to get out of Dodge."

"Awesome plan!" Sorenson said while giving Migos and Savage a fist bump.

"Whatever we find, we split evenly six ways," I said.

"Don't we have to pay a tax to the Philippine government?" Migos asked.

"We're supposed to, but after that demo goes off, we're not going to want to have a record of ever having been here. Why don't we just donate to a Philippine charity instead?"

"Don't get too far ahead of yourself. For all we know, the only thing on that wreck is a bunch of old metal cannons that set the magnetic sensors off on the AUV," McDonald added.

"That's true; in fact, it's probably the most likely scenario. We'll know more after today," I said.

CHAPTER 6

SOUTH CHINA SEA

S ORENSON DROPPED THE lime green ROV into the water from the hydraulic ramp. Next to him on the starboard side was a pole holding a pully. Playing out through the pulley was a thin green tether line attached to the ROV. The tether line was released automatically by the spool and was connected to a rugged laptop, manned by McDonald, that was the ROV's control unit. The Seabotix LBV 300 weighs thirty-nine pounds and is brick shaped with dimensions of 24 x 15 x 15 inches. The submersible robot has six thrusters, three cameras and a grabber arm underneath that can lift twenty pounds.

All of us were crowded on the sofas inside the salon. The big screen TV was streaming the video from the control unit manned by McDonald. A bright spotlight and the ROV's main camera were directed at the wall as the ROV descended. The ROV was rated to a depth of three hundred meters and on the big reel we had six hundred meters of line. McDonald and Cheryl were both wearing wetsuits, clearly hoping we would find something worth getting wet over. The camera showed a sea cliff teaming with sea life. The depth reading on the screen showed 260 feet. McDonald tilted the ROV to capture the shelf on the sea cliff below the vehicle. He moved the ROV along the shelf until it was over the sunken wreck.

Plants, coral, and sand covered the wreck, but the shape of a ship underneath was unmistakable. McDonald hovered the ROV five feet above the ship and inspected the top side. The stumps of three masts could be seen as could an elevated structure that had probably once been an upper deck containing rooms on one end of the wreck. McDonald brought the ROV over to the side of the wreck and conducted an inspection of the hull. The wood must have rotted badly over the years because the distance between the top deck and the solid rock of the shelf was only about five feet. The hull had pancaked as the wood rotted and the weight of the deck crushed down on itself.

"Whatever cargo the wreck carried is between the shelf floor and the wooden deck," I said.

"It can't be much of a cargo, because it's all flattened," McDonald said.

"Can you use the grabber to pull off the rotted decking?" I asked.

McDonald maneuvered the ROV to one end of the ship.

"How long is the ship?" I asked.

"It's about seventy feet," McDonald said

"From the shape and because of where we are it must be a junk. I wonder how old it is."

"No idea on the age. We need to find something we can use to date it."

The video showed the claw arm closing on a piece of coral and then lifting it away. Beneath a small piece of wood was visible. The claw then closed on the wood and pulled. The rotten wood pulled away like it was made of something soft.

"This is taking too long. Let's put Cheryl and McDonald in the water. Migos, you take over the ROV," I said

Savage and Sorenson helped rig up McDonald and Cheryl. Cheryl was wearing her yellow wetsuit; the dive wasn't deep enough to require a drysuit and the water temperature according to the ROV was sixty-six degrees. Minutes later, the ROV screen showed McDonald and Cheryl coming into view above the wreck. They began to pick through the debris created by the ROV on one end of the junk. Cheryl held up a bowl in front of the ROV camera, placed the bowl in a mesh bag and continued to dig. McDonald brought out a small cannon about the size of a small mortar from the debris. For the next forty minutes, the two pulled off parts of the deck, foraged beneath, and then moved on another five feet or so towards the far end. Both had a handful of items stuffed in their bags, mostly pottery or small metal items. The plan called for them to return after fifty-five minutes into the dive. That way the decompression would only be twenty minutes.

When they were ten feet from the end, McDonald held up a gold coin for us to see. It was about the size of a silver dollar and it had a square hole in the center. Cheryl joined him and soon she was holding up coins. McDonald found a bar of gold; it was a strange looking bar, not evenly shaped. At this point, all four of us in the salon of the yacht were cheering. The alarm must have gone off on their dive computers because both suddenly stopped working and began to ascend. We were a triumphant group when we brought Cheryl and McDonald back on board.

Twenty-one coins and three gold bars were in the bags.

"There's gold everywhere we looked at that far end of that wreck," McDonald announced.

"Tomorrow we'll start the salvage operation. How many of those gold bars are down there?" I asked.

"Hundreds of both. It's a major find. The boat was Chinese; the coins are from all over. The bars are all marked on the bottom in Chinese and they're stamped with the words 'ten tael'," Cheryl said.

"What's a tael?" I asked.

"It's a Chinese measurement of weight. A tael is 1.3 ounces."

"That's a lot of gold!" Migos said.

"We have enough lift bags and heavy nets to bring them up. Tomorrow we'll drop the tanks, bags, and cargo nets, and start bringing that stuff up," I said.

We worked hard the next two days, finishing the demolition sites and recovering the gold from the mystery shipwreck. The next day out, Migos and I went to work arming the demolition sites with our sleds. We were using Rheinmetall Privia limpet mines to detonate the explosive caches. The electronic timing function on the Privia allowed us to synchronize the detonation clock on all five mines so they all would explode simultaneously. We set the mines to explode at three in the afternoon, the next day.

We arrived at the first cave and I removed the first mine from its backpack. The mine is shaped like the bottom six inches of a cone and is the diameter of a large dinner plate. The Privia mines are rated to BAR-5, which is 150 feet in depth, and we were going to employ them at more than twice the recommended limit. This was a CIA plan and I just assumed the agency received a guarantee from the company that the mines would still function at the depths we were working. I used the magnetic contact to connect the mine to the nearest cargo pod and then I turned the nob to arm it. A light flashed green two times, signaling it was properly armed.

Migos and I raced from demolition point to demolition point. The sleds were operating on autopilot and to keep our masks from flying off at the high speed we had to keep our heads buried down and our bodies low inside the protected compartment, behind the nose of the sled. It took less than forty-five minutes to cover the ten miles, leapfrogging from demolition point to demolition point.

We did all of our decompression without the benefit of the ship's anchor line to guide us. We stayed on the sleds and moved from fixed depth to fixed depth while slowly making our way back to the *Sam Houston*. When we finished our marathon five-hour dive, the treasure hunters had already finished for the day. I guided my STIDD sled up onto the submerged hydraulic ramp and waited for Migos to do the same behind me. Finally, we broke the surface and four sets of hands helped to remove my mask, fins, and closed-circuit rig.

On the floor of the stern deck were two long rows of gold bars.

"Did you get everything up from the wreck?" I asked the group.

"Not even close. We think this is less than half," replied McDonald.

"How much did you recover?" I asked.

"Two hundred and sixty bars and we're still counting the coins, but it's over two thousand," McDonald said.

"That's incredible. Can we finish tomorrow by noon?" I asked.

"Yes, all we'll need will be three shifts of two of us down working and four up here receiving and unloading. We can get it done," McDonald said.

"Tomorrow at one, even if we don't have everything, we're pulling up anchor and heading back to Cyprus," I said.

I hadn't provided any updates to Mike since we departed Cyprus; we had been on a total communications blackout. I sent an encrypted message over the satphone that included the code word meaning the detonation would occur at three pm tomorrow. The message was, "Return voyage begins tomorrow."

The next morning, we were in the water as soon as the sun came up at six-twenty. The plan was to dive in three shifts of two with the duration of each dive set at two hours. Migos and I were the first ones in the water. It was our first time diving the wreck, but we had reviewed the set-up on the ROV data recordings.

We brought down four fresh air cylinders, eight lifting bags, and eight cargo nets. Once we got to the wreck we went right to work. We set up a cargo net next to the area we were going to clean and then we began to search and stack our finds onto the net. The work was easy; first, we pulled off the coral and sea life and then the deck wood. Once we removed the deck wood, what we found underneath was all loose gold coins and bars.

Each lifting bag could bring one hundred pounds of gold to the surface. The ROV would bring us a tether line that we would attach to the cargo net, then we would stick the hose from the air cylinder in and inflate the bag until it was three-quarters full. Then, we just released the bag and let it rise. The air in the bag expanded and vented as it ascended. We managed to send up two loads and were more than half done with the third when we hit our time limit.

By the time Sorenson and Savage were done, we had almost completely cleaned the wreck of gold. Cheryl and McDonald went down to finish up, while the four of us finished moving all of the treasure downstairs into the engine room. I was coming up from below deck when I noticed a ship on the horizon. Migos was monitoring the ROV and Sorenson and Savage were pulling a tether line connected to the last haul in a lifting bag that had just surfaced. I went to the wheelhouse to get my binoculars. I turned on the radar and fixed the location of the ship at five miles to our due west. Through my binoculars, I could tell it was a warship and that it was heading towards us. It was too far away to identify the flag it was flying.

"Migos, tell Cheryl and McDonald to come up right away!" I yelled. I knew Migos would then fly the ROV to them and issue the abort signal which was to move the arm left and right repeatedly until receiving a thumbs-up acknowledgment from the divers.

When the warship got within two miles, I received a broadcast on the marine channel.

"Unknown ship, this is Chinese Navy Frigate 811; prepare to be boarded."

"Chinese Navy Frigate 811 this is civilian yacht, *Day Trader*, with a Singapore registration. We are inside Philippine territorial waters and will not be subject to a Chinese inspection," I said.

"*Day Trader,* this Chinese Navy Frigate 811; you are located in Chinese waters. What is your purpose?"

"We are a pleasure craft and we are on a diving trip." The ship slowed as it came to within a mile of us.

"We are going to board and inspect your boat. Do not resist." The Chinese frigate came to a stop. I watched them slowly lower a tender from the deck down into the water. The grey warship was less than a thousand yards away. It seemed like an eternity, but Cheryl and McDonald finally broke the surface. Sorenson and Savage had already stowed the last haul of gold in the engine room. I had retrieved the anchor while I was waiting for the divers to return. I started both engines and hit full throttle. I aimed the *Sam Houston* directly toward Palawan Island thirteen miles to our east.

It takes only twenty seconds for an Azimuth 64 to get to 34 knots and that gave us a big jump start.

"*Day Trader,* heave to, or we will open fire."

"Chinese Frigate, attacking an unarmed civilian pleasure craft in Philippine waters is a war crime. We have been advised to move to the protection of the Philippines authorities. You are breaking the law." The tiny Chinese tender boat was at full throttle in pursuit, but it was futile. We were outrunning the tender. The frigate joined the chase.

I was at full speed racing toward Palawan. My navigation system showed we were well inside Philippine waters and only eight miles from land. Suddenly, an explosion and a geyser of water erupted two hundred yards in front of us. I banked the yacht to the right.

"*Day Trader,* this is Chinese Frigate 811. Heave to or the next cannon round will be aimed at your vessel."

I cut the throttle.

"Chinese Frigate 811, we have stopped. I have to warn you that we are in Philippine waters and you are in violation of international law." It took another ten minutes, but the tender once again came into view, it was two thousand yards behind and slowly closing. The menacing frigate swiftly moved back onto station a thousand yards off our stern.

It was a desperate situation and I was considering my options. None of them were good. My best idea was to rig the *Sam Houston* for destruction and try to make an underwater run to the Palawan coast using the sleds before the Chinese tender arrived.

"Chinese Frigate 811, this is Philippine Navy Frigate *Andre Bonifacio*; you are violating Philippine territorial waters. We are ordering you to leave," a voice said in accented English over the radio. This began a discussion that lasted a full thirty minutes as the Chinese frigate captain explained to the Philippine Navy captain that he was only in Philippine waters because he was pursuing us. I couldn't hear the conversation that followed, because the two military vessels moved the conversation to a different frequency. I was relieved when I watched the tender return to the Chinese frigate.

The standoff lasted a long time. I kept checking the clock display on the top of the wheelhouse console. We were at the end of the standoff because the tender was being loaded when three o'clock hit. We were located just over five miles from the nearest detonation site. Everyone was searching for a sign of a detonation, but we had no way of telling at first if the limpet mines worked. At ten minutes after three, we felt a small tremor— little more than a vibration. At three-twenty, the Chinese Frigate recovered the tender and departed, heading west at full speed. The Philippine ship never got any closer than two miles to us. I watched on the radar as it turned around and headed due east toward Palawan.

I set a course for Singapore. The entire team was in the salon watching the news on satellite. They were surfing the Philippine and Vietnamese TV stations. There was no tsunami warning broadcast, which caused us to believe the mission was a bust. More importantly, even after we had been underway for several hours, there were no tsunamis reported in the news—not in the Philippines and not in Vietnam or China.

We were still in blackout communications as per Mike's instructions, so I didn't call him and make a report. Instead, we spent the next nine days working our way back to Paphos, Cyprus. When we docked in Cyprus, we shuttled back and forth in our SUVs and moved all of the treasure to our hangar at the airport. Because of some really bad security breaches in the recent past, our hangar security is first class. We stored the booty in Cheryl's office in the Clearwater wing of the hangar. The Clearwater headquarters is a SCIF; its walls are made of reinforced steel and it's protected by a state-of-the-art security system. I thought that would be a good place to keep the treasure until we had time to figure out what it was worth and what we were going to do with it.

I found Cheryl in her office. She was in a running suit, sitting at her desk working on the computer.

"What are you up to?" I asked.

"I'm going to try to find out the name of the ship we got this gold from."

"How are you going to do that?"

"First, I'm going to date the items we brought up, and

once I know the period, I can begin to research historical records for lost ships in the area."

"How long is that going to take?"

"I don't know. I've never done this before."

"McDonald is going to clean and catalog everything. That's going to take weeks. It's a good project; it'll keep everyone busy for a good while."

"What about you?"

"I'm flying in two hours; I have a meeting with Mike."

"Where?"

"London."

CHAPTER 7

LONDON, UK

I CHECKED IN AT the Dorchester Hotel at a little after seven. I had just finished unpacking when Mike knocked on the door. He was looking officious in a dark suit and he caught me in a bear hug as he stepped into the room. He threw his overcoat on top of a chair in the hallway.

"Can I get you a drink?" I asked.

"Definitely," Mike said as he walked over to the bar in the suite's living room. He pointed to a bottle of Macallan Scotch and I fixed it for him, neat. I opened a Heineken beer for myself, as we were about to do a mission debrief which meant I was going to do a lot of talking. Mike sat on the couch and removed his shoes. I took the chair on the opposite side of the coffee table.

"Before I start, can you tell me what happened? Was the mission a success?" I asked.

"You don't know?"

"I know we positioned the charges correctly and I know

they went off, but we couldn't find any reports on what happened afterward."

"The charges went off as planned. A minor earthquake was detected along the Wa-nu fault line. A big block from the continental sea wall sheared off and slid down into the depths of the Palawan Trench and, just as predicted, a section of the fault punched up from the ocean floor. A tsunami warning was issued to all coastal areas in the southernmost region of the South China Sea. Everything went almost exactly as the simulation portrayed. Three waves pulsed west toward the Spratlys and the west coast of Vietnam. The first wave reached Mischief Reef Island in forty-seven minutes. We have satellite images of the event; the height of the wave was estimated at twenty-five feet. The first wave swept completely over the island and by the time the third wave arrived fifteen minutes later, there were no structures standing. In fact, not one part of the man-made island was above the surface. The same situation played out with every one of the island bases. The force of the tsunami scoured everything above the water line, which makes sense because it was only soft sand to begin with. The tsunami drill the Chinese had in place called for the personnel on the tiny islands to seek shelter on the ships at dock. They had enough warning to react. Most of the Chinese military personnel and all of the ships went unharmed. There were some casualties, but we don't know how many.

"The wave continued westward after it cleared the Spratlys. By the time it reached mainland China and Vietnam, it was too weak to do any serious damage. The mission was a major success. A US Naval Carrier Strike Group is now in the area and there's nothing the Chinese

Navy can do about it. The fighter aircraft that were forward positioned on those three reef island airbases are now at the bottom of the sea. The air defenses are wiped out and the sub and surface ship docks are gone. Wiping out those island bases was a game changer."

I spent the next ninety minutes telling my side of the story and answering questions. Mike was recording the debriefing and it was a pretty upbeat discussion. When I told him about the treasure, his demeanor changed, and the questions came rapid fire. When we got to the part about the stand-off with the Chinese and the Philippine Navy, I could tell from the pulse in his forehead and how he was leaning forward in his seat that he was very agitated.

"Do the Chinese suspect the tsunami was a man-made event?" I asked.

"We don't think so. The Chinese being able to pinpoint your boat above ground zero a short time before the event is definitely going to be a red flag."

"The boat was false flagged."

"With luck and some research, they could still trace it to you. If the items you pulled from the wreck are traceable to the wreck and you put them on the market, that might also provide them a lead."

"What am I supposed to do with the gold?"

"I'm not sure. For the time being, don't do anything with the treasure, until we evaluate the risks."

"Ok."

"You need to get rid of your boat."

"Why?"

"What happens if the Chinese get curious about the boat that was right above the earthquake that generated the tsunami? They'll have photos from the encounter with the Chinese frigate. Your behavior must have appeared very suspicious. If they try to find the boat in Singapore and they don't, that'll create even more suspicion. If they do a full search for every Azimut 64 in the world, your name is eventually going to pop up. When you bought that boat, you weren't even working for us; I'm sure you bought it out in the open. Getting rid of the boat won't solve the problem completely, but it'll make their work harder."

"That was really bad luck a Chinese patrol came by on the last day. I kept the radar off because I didn't want to telegraph our location, but it's also why they were able to get so close undetected."

"If you'd departed the area the day before, they wouldn't have found you anchored over the demolition site."

"Gold fever got the best of me."

"It did. Hopefully, they don't trace the boat to you and the only thing they uncover about the boat is that the crew was treasure hunting. Finding a buried treasure in international waters is a perfectly understandable reason to behave as suspiciously as you did, so it's a bad news, good news story."

"When the Chinese look into it, they'll think I was running away to avoid inspection because of the gold and not because of anything else."

"Yeah, possibly. But if they connect the boat to you, it's a certainty they'll know it was a CIA operation. You're working status with us is not a secret to them and I doubt they're going to believe the CIA was over that spot treasure hunting."

"If the Chinese learn we were the ones who destroyed their island bases, what are they going to do about it?"

"That's a question we gave a lot of thought to before going ahead with the operation. The consensus is that publicly, they won't do anything. There's no benefit to be gained by acknowledging such a huge strategic defeat. They'll retaliate, but it'll be covert, and not a major military engagement they can't win."

"Are you hungry?" I asked.

"Is that your way of saying you've had enough debrief?"

"No, I'm just really hungry. I had enough debrief two hours ago. Let's get some food. What do you feel like?"

"Seafood."

"How about beef? There's a pretty good steakhouse in this hotel. Wolfgang Puck."

"You don't want seafood?"

"Not especially—too much sea lately. You should try a week of four-hour long daily decompressions sometime. Nobu is half a block down the street. What about Asian?"

"Nobu it is."

CHAPTER 8

BEIJING, CHINA

COLONEL HUANG LEIU waited patiently in the
waiting room outside Admiral Wu's office. His
meeting with the head of the Peoples Liberation
Army Navy (PLAN) was scheduled at the request of his boss,
the Minister of State Security. Under the circumstances, he
expected the PLAN Commander to be hostile, but given the
top-level interest in the investigation, he also anticipated
reluctant compliance. The Chinese president was rumored
to have flown into a rage while reading the final tsunami
report that had been produced by PLAN. Dissatisfied
with the conclusion and recommendations of the PLAN
report, President Ping personally directed the Ministry of
State Security (MSS) to conduct a separate investigation.
Moments later, the Minister of State Security called Huang
into his office and at two o'clock that very morning, he gave
him a set of very simple instructions.

"Seven islands do not simply disappear. Find out if they
were properly built. If they were not properly built, find
out why. Were substandard materials used? If so, why? Was

it because of corruption? Was the design flawed? Was a flaw in the design concealed to avoid embarrassment? Look into every possibility for why those islands disappeared and then figure out who is to blame."

"Yes, Minister."

"Look into the geology. Should the Navy have prepared better for a tsunami risk? What was the probability of a tsunami? What were the considerations and preparations?"

"Yes, Minister."

"I have this report signed by Admiral Wu that concludes that everything was done properly, that it wasn't possible to predict the disaster. It claims the area is one of the most geologically stable zones on earth. He claims the earthquake was a one-in-a-million freak event— that it was a force of nature that could not have been predicted or prevented. Start your investigation with Admiral Wu. Find out why he is so sure of these claims, and get to the bottom of this tragedy that has set our Silk Road strategy back twenty-five years."

"Yes, Minister."

"We were only months from beginning the deployment of the J20 fighter to our naval bases in the South China Sea. The J20 is a fifth-generation stealth fighter that would have given us uncontested dominance over the region. Instead, we have now an American Aircraft Carrier Strike Force operating in the middle of our territorial waters and we're powerless to stop them. The impending timeline of the J20 deployment, the destruction of our island naval bases, and the American Navy deployment all happening at the same time is too much to just be a simple coincidence."

"Yes, Minister."

"The President is depending on MSS to find the truth. He believes the military will cover up any wrongdoing on their part. Prove him right."

"Yes, Minister."

A few hours later, Huang arrived at his appointment with the Chinese Naval Commander. Huang was outwardly calm and composed as he sat in the Admiral's waiting area. An average- looking man of medium stature, wearing a poorly tailored black suit with a white shirt and red tie, he looked like any other Chinese Government functionary. Huang was the son of a dirt farmer from an impoverished northern province. It was athletics that enabled him to escape from a lifetime of backbreaking manual labor and the crucible of hunger that, despite China's historic economic advances, still persisted in the population of four hundred million who lived in the countryside.

Huang's gymnastics potential drew the attention of the Chinese National Athletic Association while he was still only an elementary school student. After being removed from his familiar rural surroundings and family, he spent the better part of a decade intensely training as he climbed the rungs of the gymnastics ranking ladder. Huang eventually reached the level where he was competing internationally as a member of the Chinese National Team.

An awkward landing on a dismount from the parallel bars ended his gymnastics career during the Olympic tryouts. It wasn't a dramatic injury, just a simple ACL tear that prevented him from ever competing again at an Olympic level. Huang was well liked by the coaching staff and the committee members who oversaw the Chinese National Team. Being an elite athlete opened up a world to the poor farmer that his parents could never have dreamed of. Not wanting to ever return to plowing fields behind an ox, Huang leveraged his friendships and his elevated status as a member of the National Gymnastics Team and was granted admission to Beijing University.

Huang graduated first in his mechanical engineering class and, upon graduation, was screened and selected as an agent in the Ministry of State Security. The same intelligence, dedication, and hard work that made him an athletic and academic success also served him well in his career. MSS was a magnet for engineering and science majors because its primary task was corporate espionage. Much of China's newfound economic and military strength is the result of intellectual property theft from the West and MSS has been at the center of that effort. Huang soon found himself very adept at finding clever ways to steal industrial secrets from Japan and the West. His career blossomed and not only did he make the rank of Colonel by the age of 39, but the Minister himself was now personally tasking him with highly sensitive assignments.

The outwardly calm facial expression and easy demeanor he showed to the world masked a drive and intensity few could match. Huang considered his situation. The Minister was ambitious. He would use this investigation to gain an advantage over his rival, the PLA Commander. He would also use it to gain favor with President Ping. Huang would be rewarded immensely if the investigation discovered fault with the Navy.

An aide dressed in the white uniform of a Navy captain ushered Huang into the Admiral's office. The Admiral remained seated behind his desk and did not rise to greet him. The Admiral did not acknowledge him and did not even offer him a seat. Huang gave the superior officer a slight bow and seated himself in a chair on the opposite side of the Admiral's desk.

The two men sat in silence for an uncomfortably long period of time. Finally, Huang broke the ice.

"Admiral, I realize President Ping's order to the Minister of State Security to conduct a follow-up investigation on the incident in the South China Sea is not something you deem necessary. I'm very certain your personnel did a thorough investigation and produced an impeccable report. Please understand, this assignment is not of my making; I have been placed in a difficult situation. I wish only to complete a review of the findings from your report and return to my daily duties."

"Do you have a copy of the Naval Report?" asked the Admiral.

"No sir, I do not."

The Admiral pressed the intercom on his phone and directed his aide to make a copy of the report and bring it into the office.

"You shall have a copy immediately. The report is classified, and I will trust you to treat it accordingly."

"Of course."

"And can I expect regular updates on your investigation?"

"Yes, I will keep you up to date on my progress. Once I review the report, I will provide your office the names of the people I would like to talk to. After I've spoken to the appropriate naval personnel, I should be able to wrap-up my review of the report quickly."

"You will have my full cooperation. Contact my aide

directly with the names of the personnel you wish to meet; he will make the necessary arrangements."

Huang Lieu stood at attention and bowed to the Admiral.

"Thank you, sir. I've taken more than enough of your time."

"The report will be available to you outside."

Huang signed for a copy of the report at the reception desk in the Admiral's outer office. The report was three inches thick and came wrapped in a thick brown envelope.

The studious Huang went directly to his cramped office at the MSS Headquarters in Beijing. Working through the night, he read the detailed technical report cover to cover. He read it a second time and made a list of the personnel he wished to meet. Addendums to the report included a list of the naval personnel killed in the tsunami, lists of survivors, and the Chinese Navy ships that were operating in the South China Sea during the event. References were also included to the many scientists consulted in the creation of the report.

It took three months working every day and most nights for Huang Lieu to complete the arduous task of interviewing all of the key figures in the Navy report. He kept both the State Security Minister and the Navy Commander satisfied with weekly status reports. He had found nothing to contradict the Navy's conclusions. The Navy Report appeared to be complete without deception. The science was solid and the evidence that the reef islands were in a low-risk area for seismic activity irrefutable. Proper precautions had been taken, and the islands were constructed to withstand the highest levels of typhoons.

They were not made tsunami-proof, but that was never a reasonable requirement. It would have required tens of millions of square meters of sand and decades more time to build the islands high enough to withstand a ten-meter-high tsunami wave. Tsunami-proofing the islands was never a practical consideration; he could find no fault with the Navy engineers who designed and built the structures.

He had only one more task to complete before finalizing his own report. He was going to talk to the captains of the commercial and military ships operating in the general area. The report included lists of the ships assigned to the island bases as well as many eyewitness accounts from Chinese naval personnel. He intended to make a thorough analysis of every military and commercial vessel in the general area and interview as many witnesses as he could find. He flew to the naval base in Hainan to begin, and for the next two months bounced around from naval base to naval base interviewing Navy crewman from ships as they returned to port.

It was in a tiny naval base in Sri Lanka where Huang caught up with the captain of the Chinese Naval Frigate 811 named *Jiang*. The *Jiang* was not included in the appendix of the Navy's official report; he only learned of the ship from the crew of another. He ended each of his interviews with the same question. Do you know of any other ships that were operating in the area at the time of the tsunami? He had been given the name of the frigate *Jiang* from the Captain of a troop carrier.

The captain of the *Jiang* was a short thin man with the weathered face of a seasoned mariner. Huang asked him the same set of questions he had asked the previous captains regarding where they were and what they were doing at the time of the earthquake. He was surprised to learn the *Jiang* was close to the epicenter of the earthquake. He was even more surprised at the *Jiang's* confrontation with the Philippine Navy frigate and the suspicious activity of the Singapore yacht, *Day Trader*.

"Captain, during the investigation following the tsunami, did any other officer speak to you about the incident with the *Day Trader* motor yacht?"

"No, they didn't."

"Did you report to Naval Command your position and activities on that day?"

"Yes of course; it was contained in my daily report submitted to the Regional Headquarters."

"Do you still have a copy of your report and do you have any images of the *Day Trader*?"

"Yes, of course," the Captain said.

"Why did you leave the *Day Trader's* position?"

"We were inside Philippine waters. We were in a standoff with the largest warship in the Philippine Navy. We were in the process of escalating the forcefulness of our demand to inspect the *Day Trader* when we were given a flash message to proceed as quickly as possible to Fiery Cross Reef."

"Why Fiery Cross Reef?"

"To conduct search and rescue operations as necessary."

"Yes, but why Fiery Cross? There were other islands in peril."

"I don't know. I imagine the command allocated rescue assignments based on capability and proximity."

Huang's next destination was Singapore. He researched the records on the *Day Trader* and learned it was an Azimut

64 yacht, built in 2005 and registered to Stephen Chang. With further research, he learned Stephen Chang was a forty-year-old derivatives trader who lived in Singapore. In two days of searching, Huang was unable to find where Stephen Chang kept the *Day Trader* docked. Finally, he went to the apartment address he found on Stephen Chang's boat registration to ask him directly.

He managed to bypass the doorman and the lobby security guard by entering through the service elevator. The address on the boat registration and tax records showed Stephen lived in apartment 1710. Huang knocked on the door, waited a few seconds and then rang the doorbell. There was no answer. He removed a door pick from his jacket pocket, put it to work and made his way inside. At fifteen hundred square feet it was a large three-bedroom condominium by Singapore standards. He walked into the living room looking for clues. He checked the address of the mail and other documents in the apartment and they all showed it to be the residence of Neo Ling Chong. Huang couldn't find any clues during a quick search that showed how long Chong had been living in the apartment or how long it had been since Stephen Chang moved out, but one thing he knew for certain was that Stephen Chang didn't live there.

He went to the lobby and asked the doorman where he could find Stephen Chang. The doorman wasn't cooperative, even after Huang offered him money. The doorman insisted that he wasn't allowed to give away resident information and instead referred him to the property management company. Huang was growing frustrated with the level of difficulty in locating the owner of the *Day Trader*. The next night, he broke into the property management office. He conducted a download of their tenant files and then spent the next three days reviewing them. It was at this point that he became convinced that Stephen Chang didn't exist.

Huang believed that, just as in a good gymnastics routine, investigations have a rhythm to them. When you slow the pace or hurry, you can lose your balance. Sometimes, when the tempo on a particular line of inquiry started to lose momentum, he liked to pursue another line, just to maintain the tempo. He decided to shift from who the owner of the Azimut 64 was, to what the owner was doing at that particular spot.

He reviewed again the report from the captain of the frigate who had encountered the *Day Trader*. He studied the images he received from the file. Some showed that members of the crew were diving when the frigate first encountered them. Pictures of the yacht showed lots of heavy equipment and diving gear stowed at the stern of the boat. The report also verified the location of where the yacht was first encountered as being directly above the epicenter of the earthquake.

Huang's next stop was the Yulin Naval Base on the island of Hainan. He was aware that the two deep water acoustic detectors (SOSUS systems) located in Micronesia and the Marianas Trench were too far away to answer his next question, but he had another idea. Yulin Naval Base was the home of the Chinese Navy Submarine Headquarters; he was operating on a hunch that a submarine was patrolling within range of the epicenter and had an acoustic recording of the seismic event.

It took the intervention of the MSS Minister and the reluctant support of the PLAN Commander, but after an additional two weeks search, he finally got what he was looking for. His next stop was back to the geology department at his alma mater, the University of Beijing. It was during the review of the data from the Yulin Naval Base that Huang had his eureka moment. Days later, a fatigued and self-satisfied Huang made an appointment with the Minister of State Security to deliver his report.

He arrived at the Minister's office twenty minutes early. He had a classified laptop tucked under his arm and two copies of the report in a red folder marked Top Secret. The Minster's senior aide met him in the waiting room.

"I will take those and have the conference room set up. It should only be a few minutes before we begin; can you please provide the password?" the aide said, referring to Huang's laptop and report copies.

Minutes later, the aide escorted Huang into the conference room. As he entered, the first thing he noticed was how big the conference room was; he had expected a more intimate setting to brief the Minister. The next thing that caught his attention was that the large U-shaped conference table was filled with people. When he noticed that it wasn't the Minister sitting at the head of the table, that it was President Ping himself, he felt a minor tremble in his left hand and, for just a second, he was flustered. Years of performing in front of thousands of people at international gymnastics competitions taught Huang how to maintain his composure in pressure situations. He used a meditation tool from his past and gained control of his breathing. He bowed deeply to the audience and began.

"President, I beg your permission to begin," he said to President Ping, who responded with a slight nod.

"Sir, the conclusion of my report is that the destruction of all seven of our man-made island naval bases was the result of a man-made tsunami."

"That's impossible!" he heard the Peoples Liberation Army Commander blurt out. The PLA Commander was sitting to the left of the President. Huang looked into the eyes of the clearly agitated man.

"We have received your weekly updates and we have had our own scientists review your findings. What you are suggesting is impossible with any munition other than a nuclear device. If a nuclear device was detonated in the South China Sea, we would know about it; the signatures could not be hidden."

"Sir, with the greatest respect, I would like to present two elements of information that are very recent and were not included in my weekly progress reports."

"Go on," he heard the General mutter. He moved forward to the next slide of his presentation. "Sir, the seismic wave you see is from an undersea earthquake that occurred three years ago and registered a 7.2. Please listen." Huang played the sound over the speakers. "Gentlemen, please indulge me while I show you the graphs and play you the sounds of similar earthquakes." He then played nine more underwater recordings of earthquakes while showing them graphs of the single acoustic spike created by each of the tremors.

"Sir, this next recording was captured by a Shang Class Submarine located less than sixty nautical miles from the epicenter of the earthquake that destroyed our bases. Please listen." Huang played the recording three times. Then he advanced the slide.

"The image on the top is what the sound waves of the first ten earthquakes look like when graphed. Please notice the difference between those earthquakes and the one on the bottom that was used to attack us." The graphic on the bottom showed three shorter descending waves that preceded a much larger longer wave than the single spike depicted earlier.

"I've consulted with Doctor Shing Ah Chin at the University of Beijing. He is an expert on seismology, and it is his opinion that these three unusual waves that exist on our earthquake graphs are caused by an explosion. This reading is the explosion that was used to trigger the earthquake that created the tsunami.

"Let me explain these three small waves. In an underwater explosion, the first wave is a shock wave, as you see. The second, shorter wave is the cavitation pulse, and the third wave, the one you see here, that is the smallest wave and it is the bubble pulse. There is no doubt in the professor's opinion that these readings could be created by anything other than an underwater explosion.

"It is the opinion of the Doctor that sufficient explosives, perfectly placed in an area with the proper geology, could generate the seismic activity and subsequent tsunami that destroyed our bases," Huang said to a speechless group.

"He made a simulation of how the event would have happened. Before I start, let me explain what you will see. First will be the explosion along the cliff face of the continental shelf. Next is the landslide as a large portion of the shelf descends into the bottom of the sea. Next is the upward thrust that is the earthquake and it is caused by the change in pressure on the tectonic plate. This upward thrust is what sends the pulse through the water. That pulse is the tsunami." Huang hit the play button on the slide and the animated simulation of the scenario he described was shown to the silent audience.

"Additionally, I believe I have identified the boat that delivered the explosives to the target area. The images taken from the destroyer recorded a team that was diving above the epicenter. The images were too far away for facial recognition, but they clearly show technical diving equipment," Huang said as he advanced to the next slide that included an image of the *Day Trader* taken by the frigate *Jiang's* gun camera during the encounter.

"Who does that yacht belong to?" the President asked.

"Sir, the yacht was false flagged as being owned by a man named Stephen Chang from Singapore. However, I've been to Singapore and there's no *Day Trader* motor yacht and there's no Stephen Chang."

"Do we have any leads on where that yacht came from?" asked the President.

"Sir, a full investigation into finding the yacht and crew has not yet commenced. I came here today to issue an interim report on the first task I was assigned, which was to review the Navy's incident report. I believe now, we would all agree that the initial report did not reach the proper conclusion. I have ideas on how to proceed toward identifying the yacht and crew, but felt it was most important to first deliver this information."

"What is your name, agent?" the President asked.

"Sir, I am Colonel Huang Leiu."

"Excellent work, Colonel Huang," the President said as

he looked over to his right at the Minister of State Security with approval.

"Colonel, you may consider yourself dismissed, while we discuss this troubling information," the State Security Minister said.

Huang walked hurriedly to the exit in the back of the conference room. The Minister's aide followed him out as he also was dismissed.

"You have brought great credit to the Minister; he is most pleased," the aide said as the two drank tea in the outer office.

"Thank you, sir."

"What will you request when you next see the Minister?" asked the aide.

"I would like to stay on this case. I believe I can find the criminals who killed our people."

"I would bet the Ministers and the President are discussing what they will do once we find the perpetrators. It will not be good for them."

"Will we go to war?" asked Huang.

"No, I don't believe so. We will hunt the criminals down like dogs and kill them in a most public and spectacular way. We will show the Americans that we know what they have done and provide them with an example to understand the level of our rage. I don't think we are prepared to go to war against the American military at this time."

"I also suspect it's the Americans. The images of the divers looked to be American, but that is yet to be proven. We will have to see where the facts take us."

Huang stayed in the Minister's outer office for almost three hours while the security leadership of China deliberated in private. Finally, the outer doors of the conference room opened, and the men inside began to flow out. President Ping was the first to exit. Huang stood by the aide and waited for the Minister.

Soon he was in the Minister's inner office, seated across the desk from his boss.

"All eyes are on the Ministry of State Security to see how we handle this next task," the Minister said as he lit a cigarette.

"The failure of the Peoples Liberation Army has elevated us to new heights in the eyes of the President; we must not fail."

"We won't, Minister."

"Your work so far has been impressive. Finding the boat and the crew is going to require more personnel than just yourself. We'll construct a task force. You will, of course, lead this task force. I want you to know, whatever you need, you will get. This is our top priority. We must find the men who attacked China and we must retaliate in such a way that the Americans or whoever was behind this attack understand that we will not be trifled with."

"Yes, sir."

"You must be very tired. I'm sure you barely slept last night. I knew you had big news and that is why I invited all of the members of the Security Council. I didn't want to give anyone the opportunity to alter the report. I thought it best for you to deliver it directly to the President. Go home, get rest. Come back tomorrow morning with a list of what you will need to accomplish this next mission."

"Yes sir, thank you, sir."

CHAPTER 9

PAPHOS, CYPRUS

I RETURNED FROM LONDON and went directly to the Trident hangar. I found Cheryl and the rest of the team hard at work cleaning, sorting, and cataloging the treasure. A white tarp on top of Cheryl's thick office rug was lined with gold bars sorted by origin and age. Some were Chinese, others were from other parts of Asia and Europe. The Clearwater conference table in the adjacent room had gold coins all separated into different categories.

"Did anyone figure out the name of the junk yet?" I asked the group.

"Not yet. We have David Forrest and ALICE working on it." ALICE is the supercomputer-powered program Clearwater uses for its core business, which is to track commercial ships for insurance companies and shipping lines. Trident occasionally uses ALICE's unique capabilities for intelligence purposes. The US Government feeds ALICE with classified data feeds and imagery when our missions require it. When the mission doesn't require it, ALICE relies on open source data. ALICE was developed by David Forrest, the Chair of the Edinburgh

College Computer Science Department and the co-owner of Clearwater. Trident is the other Clearwater owner.

"Does that mean you've read David Forrest into the operation?" I asked Cheryl.

"Yes, I did. I've also tasked him to concentrate on counterintelligence—to give us early warning if anyone is looking for us or the *Sam Houston*."

"How will he do that?"

"He has real-time access to intel feeds that include electronic communications and internet searches. If someone starts a search for us, he'll be notified."

"Yeah, that's good. You're thinking along the same lines as Mike. I have to scuttle the *Sam Houston* tonight."

"He's that worried?"

"He wasn't happy we stayed in the area a day more than we had to and recovered the gold."

"The plan called for us to stay in the area until the day we detonated the charge to safeguard the area; what's he complaining about?"

"Running into that Chinese Navy frigate was a horrible stroke of bad luck. It doesn't matter whether we were following orders, or we got stupid because of gold fever. Either way, the Chinese will be looking for the boat, which is why I need to get rid of it."

"Need some help, boss?" Migos asked.

"Yeah, I need to take some things off the boat, then tonight I'll take it out and scuttle it and return with the tender."

"What about the registration on the *Sam Houston*? We need to destroy the records," Cheryl said.

"Mike's already done that; he had the Agency call in a favor with the Bahamian government."

"Weather better be good, that tender's not designed for rough seas," said McDonald.

"Forecast is good. Speaking of waves, did you see any satellite photos of our handiwork?" I asked.

"We got it from Clearwater. The islands were wiped clean," Migos said.

"What about the collateral damage? Mike told me there was none; is that confirmed by Clearwater?"

"It is. The hardest hit area was in Vietnam and the wave was barely noticeable as anything more than a rogue. No damage to people or property."

"So, the only people coming after us will be the Chinese, then," I said.

"And maybe the ghosts of whoever this gold used to belong to," McDonald said.

"How much is there?"

"Most of the bars and coins are denominated in tael. We recovered 61,241 tael. In ounces, that's 81,645. At today's rate that's a little over one hundred million dollars. The thing is, all of the coins are from the eighteenth and nineteenth centuries, they're in good shape, and many of them are collectors' items. We found one coin that alone is worth over five hundred thousand dollars."

"What do you think all of this is worth?" I asked McDonald with the sweep of my hand.

"Between two hundred million and five hundred million."

"That's a big spread; any ideas of what to do with it?" I asked.

"We're going to take another week to classify everything and value it based on what we find on the internet. Then we're going to split it into six equally valued piles and we're going to randomly assign each person their share by drawing numbers out of a hat," McDonald said.

"That's fine with me. But for at least the next six months, nobody should do anything. Park your share in a bank vault and don't put anything on the market. We need to stay under the Chinese radar," I said.

"The Chinese won't know we found treasure," Migos said.

"We don't know that. That Chinese frigate had powerful cameras and we don't know what they recorded. It could be the way they trace the tsunami back to us."

I left the hangar with Migos. We both drove SUVs, so we could offload as much as possible from the yacht. The two of us worked all afternoon, each making six trips back to the hangar with stuff. I had a pizza dinner with the team in the Trident hangar. All of the guys were in a great mood. Sorenson, Savage, Migos, and McDonald had all just become instantly rich and the rush that came from discovering a shipwreck with a fortune inside still hadn't left them.

We were in the fenced-in kitchen area inside the cavernous Trident hangar. The guys were all seated around a big picnic table on benches drinking beer and pulling slices of pizza from open boxes. I was drinking a diet Coke leaning against the stainless-steel refrigerator door near the back wall when Cheryl came over.

"Are you sad about your boat?" she asked.

"I am."

"Want me to come with you?"

"No, I want to say goodbye to the *Sam Houston* alone."

"You can buy another one."

"I have a lot of great memories on that boat. Remember our first night together? It was docked in the Dubai Marina and you were still a Chinese spy, using your body to extract secrets from me. It was my home for years. I hate to kill it."

"It's not a living thing—it's just a boat, and I wasn't using my body to extract secrets."

"You were using your feminine wiles to manipulate me, and it worked."

"It still works, big boy," Cheryl said with a smile.

The sea was calm. There was no wind. It was a cool, moonless night. I left the Paphos Marina on a heading that was due south for twenty miles. I steered the boat from the helm station on my favorite place on the boat, which was the flydeck. Fifteen feet above the waterline, I had a great view of the yacht and surrounding waters. The Mediterranean is deep, over forty-seven hundred feet in some places. Where I stopped was, according to the charts, over twelve hundred feet deep. I took the satchel next to me, went down two flights of stairs to the lower deck, and placed two charges in the floor of the engine room and a third charge at the bow of the yacht. On the floor of the owner's stateroom, I tamped the charges to direct the blast downward through the hull. I used a ten-minute time fuse connected to a non-electric blasting cap that was stuck into the end of a one-and-a-quarter-pound stick of C-4. Once I pulled the igniter on all three charges, I hustled up the stairs and into the tender perched on the hydraulic ramp in the stern. I lowered the tiny thirteen-foot tender into the dark waters, started the outboard and positioned myself about a hundred yards from the *Sam Houston's* starboard.

I didn't have to wait long. The charge in the bow of the

yacht went off first. Seconds later, the two in the engine room went off in rapid succession. The boat's structure above the waterline remained intact, but underneath, the newly formed holes must have quickly flooded the yacht. I watched the *Sam Houston* sink fast into the dark waters. It was gone in less than five minutes. As soon as the flybridge slipped under the water, I offered a salute to my old friend, turned the tender north and headed back to Paphos.

The next morning, I left the gold bugs to finish the inventory and flew to Edinburgh, Scotland with Cheryl. We landed in a snowstorm. We had a car take us to the Balmoral in downtown Edinburgh where we were staying. I thought Cheryl would like the Balmoral because it's in the downtown shopping area near the Castle. I always use it, because it's near David's office at the University. David was in the lobby waiting for us when we entered. We shook the snow off our coats and greeted him warmly. After we checked in, the bellhop took our luggage upstairs and the three of us went downstairs to "Scotch," the appropriately named hotel whisky bar.

"It's not even December yet and we're having a blizzard," David said.

"I noticed. Whatever happened to global warming?" I asked.

"Still a possibility, but it's the sun. We're at a point of record low sunspot activity," David said.

"Is it the end of times?" I said jokingly.

"No, just a cycle called the solar minimum."

"If it's the apocalypse, then this is the place to be. Five hundred different whiskies, we won't even notice the end," I said to David as he smiled and lit his pipe.

Later, while David and I were enjoying a rare Mortlach Scotch and Cheryl a ginger lemon tea, the topic turned to the purpose of our visit.

"What have you learned about our shipwreck?" I asked.

"ALICE has been busy. We've searched every digitized maritime record in Asia."

"But did you learn anything?"

"Quite a bit. I'm reasonably convinced the junk you discovered was the *Red Dragon* which sank in 1809. It was part of a fleet headed by the famous Pirate Queen Ching Shih, later known as Lady Chang.

"Lady Chang commanded the largest pirate force in world history—seventeen hundred junks and as many as seventy thousand men. When China opened up to European trade at the end of the 18th century, the rampant pirate problem was an annoyance that had to be dealt with. In 1809, the Europeans stepped in to defeat the pirates who were stifling trade.

"It was because of the Portuguese involvement that I was able to find a record of the lost junk. The bulk of Lady Chang's fighting force, including her husband, were trapped by the Portuguese and the Emperor's navies. Terms of surrender and pardon were agreed to and Lady Chang traveled to Palawan Island where she kept part of her booty hidden in a cave. She retrieved the bounty and divided it among three junks. It was typhoon season and she took extra as an insurance policy. She lost the *Red Dragon* off the coast of Palawan when they were hit by a cyclone."

"How much was the ransom?"

"It was 130,000 tael."

"Each ship would have carried sixty-five thousand tael,

which is consistent with what we found. What did you learn about the *Red Dragon*?"

"It was built in the late 1700s as a commercial freighter and it exchanged hands a few times after it was captured by pirates. Eventually, all pirates in the region pledged to Lady Chang, and so it would have come under her command sometime after 1804. That's all I know."

"That's a lot. How's the counterintelligence effort going?" I asked.

"Lots of inquiries for the *Day Trader* and Stephen Chang from Singapore. Mostly from mainland China. Lists of Azimut 64 yacht owners and maintenance records and parts shipments from service providers, manufacturers, and parts distributors are all being compiled by Chinese Intelligence. Insurance companies are being checked for boat coverage on an Azimut 64. If it hasn't already, the *Sam Houston* and Pat Walsh are eventually going to make it onto one of those Chinese lists."

"Those must be very big lists."

"Only 217 Azimut 64s have ever been manufactured. It's not that big of a list."

"Once my name comes up, the Chinese will know it was me."

"Yes, they know who Pat Walsh is and they know who you work for. You'll be the top suspect."

"They won't be able to prove it was me."

"They won't be able to prove it in a court of law, but this isn't a court case we're talking about."

"In your opinion, the Chinese are definitely going to figure out it was me."

"Yes, you've been to too many ports, made too many

refueling stops and repairs to hide the association from the Chinese. It's a data analysis exercise and just a matter of time before they crunch the numbers and identify you."

"Even if they know it was me, so what? Building naval bases in international waters and claiming the territory and all of the natural resources that come with it isn't exactly legal either. If they have a problem with what we did they should take it up with the US Government."

"I don't know what the Chinese will do. But I'm sure they will do something severe," Cheryl said.

"You need to disappear. Once the Chinese start looking at me, they're going to find you and that could be dangerous," I said to Cheryl.

"Where should I go?"

"Langley, you're safest inside a CIA safe house."

"I've gone that route before, and I don't want to repeat it. I've given this some thought. I think we should go to the Bahamas."

"Why?"

"The house is easily fortified and defended; it would take a major military-style assault to penetrate. We'll get early warning because we'll know immediately if a group of Chinese land on the island because they'll stick out like a sore thumb. I'd feel safer and more comfortable there than in a CIA safe house."

"We'll consult Mike. See what he thinks."

"In the meantime, we'll stash the pirate loot and move our gunfighters to Eleuthera."

"That works for me."

"Can you provide ISR once we get to Eleuthera?" I asked David.

"I'll put in a request as soon as we're done."

"What else can you tell us about this Pirate Queen?" I asked David.

"Quite a bit. I've done considerable reading over the past few days."

"Why don't you stay for dinner. I have a booking at the Number 1 upstairs. We can order the tasting menu, get the matching wines, and you can fill us in on this pirate wench."

David held our attention for the next three hours with stories of the pirate queen. He's a brilliant man with an amazing memory. The Balmoral clock tower atop the hotel struck ten when we were putting David into a car to send him home. The snow had stopped, and the empty street was so quiet we could hear the echo of the bells off the surrounding buildings.

"That clock's been three minutes fast since it was built in 1902. I read that in the brochure," I said to Cheryl

"Why not fix it?"

"This place was originally built by a railroad; the clock was set three minutes fast so that people wouldn't miss their trains next door at the Waverley Place train station. Now it's kept that way out of tradition."

Cheryl and I retired to our room. I went to the window and pulled open the drapes. We were in the JK Rowling Suite, where she wrote the final Harry Potter book. Outside, a fresh blanket of snow covered the grey stones of Edinburgh Castle. The only light came from a couple of streetlamps reflecting against the snow under the heavy cloud cover. Edinburgh Castle in the distance had a dark Hogwarts quality to it. It was very much in contrast to my mood which, after a Michelin starred meal, an abundance of very high-quality spirits, and the inspiration of David's tales of pirate conquest, was very upbeat.

"What do you think of the décor?" I asked.

"There's a picture of Sean Connery with Ursula Andress wearing a bikini in the bathroom," Cheryl said in a disapproving tone.

"No doubt about it; this place has class."

"Class; is that what you call it?"

"We should stay with the Bond theme. Tonight can be *The Man with the Golden Gun* night; I'll be 007 and you can play the hot Asian girl."

"How do you know there was a hot Asian girl in that movie?"

"There's a *Man with the Golden Gun* movie poster hanging in the bedroom and it has a hot Asian girl in it."

"Who played Bond?"

"Sean Connery."

"Who was the Bond girl?"

"No idea on who the actress was, but if my memory is correct, the character was named Chew Mee or something like that."

"That's horrible."

"It was a different age. This place is great—Harry Potter and James Bond themes, a super restaurant, a bar with five hundred different whiskies. If I find a pistol range in the fitness center, I'm never leaving."

"It's a bit much."

"If you think this place is too much, then I better cancel our trip to Disney World."

CHAPTER 10

BEIJING, CHINA

H UANG WORE A surgeon's mask over his face as he walked to the Ministry building. The pollution level was at its highest level in months; a pall of grey smoke hung in the air, so thick it blocked the sun. He passed through security and entered the empty elevator. His team of researchers occupied the entire eleventh floor of the high rise. When he arrived at his office, the reaction from his secretary was the first sign something was off.

"What is it, Ming?" he asked.

"The Minister is inside your office waiting for you."

"Have you brought him tea?"

"Yes, sir."

"Excellent, please have mine sent in and leave us in privacy," Huang said as he entered his office.

"Minister, it's an honor to have you visit."

'Huang, I need an update. You've done excellent work, but I'm under a lot of pressure to deliver results. I've been in the intelligence business long enough to know that pressure doesn't hasten results, but our detractors in the PLA are sowing seeds of failure to the higher-ups and I could use some good news."

"We have made progress, Minister. We don't yet have all of the answers you seek, but I can give you everything we have if you have the time."

"That would be most helpful, Colonel Huang."

"The boat used by the divers who rigged the explosions is registered in the Bahamas. The name of the yacht is the *Sam Houston*."

"How do you know?"

"From the frigate footage, we identified the vessel as an Azimut 64. Only 217 were ever built. We tracked the location of every yacht through multiple sources including insurance, boat registrations, marina records, and AIS tracking records. We narrowed down the possibilities to thirty-seven boats.

"From the thirty-seven possible, we looked into the owners. The average yacht owner is not an underwater demolition expert. The depth at the location our frigate confronted the yacht is at least sixty meters and it's close to a shelf that's over one thousand meters deep. This was a serious technical dive and not something the average wealthy retired yacht owner could perform.

"The only Azimut 64 yacht owner who fit the profile was Pat Walsh. He's a former US Army Officer and he's a CIA asset."

"How do you know?"

"He operates a company out of Abu Dhabi named Trident. He's an arms dealer who was very active during the fight against ISIS. He was and still is to some extent the CIA's conduit of weapons to the Peshmerga. He has sometimes bought from Chinese companies and he's had frequent contact with Chinese businesses and Chinese Intelligence."

"Do we have a file on him?"

"I have requested his file from Chinese Intelligence, but it hasn't been delivered yet."

"When did you make the request?"

"Yesterday afternoon."

"I'll put a rush on it. What else?"

"Trident does more than supply weapons; they are also a paramilitary organization. They conduct covert operations for the CIA."

"Like creating tsunamis in the South China Sea?"

"They would be a good choice. They're not officially part of the US Government. As contractors, they allow for deniability."

"What other names do you have?"

"The images taken from our frigate captured five personnel. We assume one more was in the wheelhouse for a total of six. We don't have a positive identity on any of the other members of Trident yet, but we're working on it."

"Where's Pat Walsh now?"

"We don't know. We tracked his yacht to a marina in Paphos, Cyprus; the yacht left the marina three days ago and hasn't returned."

"How do you know this?"

"I have people watching the marina. We interviewed the marina staff and the crew of some neighboring boats."

"How are you going to find him?"

"We're covering every marina within fuel range, we'll catch him when he stops to refuel or if he returns to Paphos."

"It would be good if you caught him. We would do well to learn more about Pat Walsh."

"Once we get the files from Intelligence, that will help."

"You will have them."

"In the meantime, we'll continue to identify the yacht crew and to find the yacht."

"You've firmly established that it was the Americans who attacked us. This was the most critical information. I'll make a report to the President."

"Yes, sir. I won't let you down."

CHAPTER 11

SWITZERLAND

WE TOUCHED DOWN in a Dassault Falcon onto a small airfield sixty miles outside of Geneva. Cheryl and I were seated across from each other as we looked out the aircraft window and watched a convoy of two armored cars led by a Mercedes sedan approach. We were high in the Alps and when the cabin door opened a bitter chill swept through the aircraft.

The men removed a steady stream of chrome metal Zargo cases from the plane's cargo compartment and moved them into the armored cars. When they finished, Cheryl and I deplaned and went to the back seat of a waiting grey Mercedes that was parked at the front of the convoy. The driver ignored us as he waited for a signal from someone to tell him the cargo was fully loaded. I saw the reflection of a hand wave in the passenger side rear view mirror and off we went.

We drove into a large offloading bay that was carved into the side of the mountain. Cheryl and I got out of the Mercedes, climbed a short set of stairs onto the loading ramp, and were met by a Swiss gentleman wearing a Russian-style fur hat and a heavy wool jacket.

"So very nice to see you again, Mr. Walsh," he said as we approached the golf cart he was standing next to.

"It's good to see you as well, Mr. Hofstadter. Thank you for arranging this deposit on such short notice."

"No trouble at all," he said, in a thick German accent.

Thirty-six cargo cases were offloaded from the two armored cars and then loaded onto four narrow flatbed cars that were pulled by an electric tug. Once everything was loaded, Mr. Hofstadter went to one of the gates on the far wall, swiped a security pass, and opened the door to passage C. Our golf cart entered the passage and drove for ten minutes deep into the mountain. We passed numerous vaults on both sides of the solid rock corridor until we reached one marked C244. I got out and went to the vault door. The door was made of stainless steel and next to it was a biometric scanner. I swiped my card and then placed my hand on the reader. When the light went from red to yellow, I pressed my forehead to the retinal scanner until I heard the clicking of the vault door unlocking. The heavy vault door came toward me and then swung open to my left.

Cheryl followed me inside the vault. The room was rectangular in shape, approximately thirty feet by sixty feet. The temperature and humidity in the room were climate controlled. Against the walls were pallets. Some held gold bars, others held stacks of currency, mostly dollars and Euros.

"What's all of this?" Cheryl asked.

"This is my rainy-day fund," I answered.

"The Vault, as they call themselves, is not a bank. It's just the most secure place in the world to keep valuables.

The three most common items are gold, currency, and art, in that order. I keep a stash here for the next time the US Government decides to freeze all of my assets."

"That's smart. I can see why you thought it would be a good place to keep our pirate treasure."

"This place is more secure than Fort Knox and there are no records or reporting requirements to any government."

"The other guys should use this place."

"Not enough time; the vetting process to get approved as a customer takes more than a year. Being a member here is not an easy club to join."

We watched the pallets on top of the flatbed cars get moved into the vault with a forklift. Once all thirty-six cases were accounted for and stored in place, I updated a hand-written inventory sheet mounted on the wall near the door and secured the vault. Our golf cart followed the tug out of the mountain. When we reached the end of the hallway, Mr. Hofstadter had to get out of the cart and open up the gateway to the loading bay. Cheryl and I got back into the Falcon and were back in the air less two hours from when we landed.

When we arrived in Eleuthera we found Migos and McDonald were already there.

"Any updates on Savage and Sorenson?" I asked.

"They're in Grand Cayman. They found a bank there willing to provide them with a safety deposit service."

"Are they still using the C130?"

"No, they sent it back after they offloaded it in Grand Cayman."

"Where does Maria have you staying?"

"We're all upstairs in the main house."

"It's going to be a lot less cramped than on that boat. At least everyone gets their own room."

"What are we supposed to be doing here, anyway?"

"Laying low, staying in a defensive mode in case the Chinese decide to retaliate against us."

"Why here?"

"It's an easy place to spot a Chinese hit squad."

"Not a lot of Chinese visitors to Eleuthera?"

"It's not on the Chinese tourism list. Busloads of them show up in Abu Dhabi in the middle of the summer when it's one hundred and thirty degrees, but so far in the Bahamas, even at peak tourist season, there are hardly any Chinese; it isn't on the Chinese travel circuit for some unknown reason."

"So that's why I get so many stares," Cheryl interjected.

"If the stares are from women, then yes. If the stares are from men, then probably not. You get leered at by guys from everywhere in the world," I said.

"What are we supposed to do while we're here?" Sorenson asked.

"We have a great beach with surfboards, boogie boards, paddle boards, and jet skis. We have an excellent gym that has enough free weights even for you. Tippy's, the best bar and restaurant on Eleuthera, is right next door. This should be a vacation. Just make sure you don't go anywhere alone and make sure you stay up on comms and that you're armed at all times."

"That's it?"

"The Trident office is down the street a couple of miles. Most of you've never met Jessica in person. It might be a good idea to stop in and meet the girl who actually pays your salaries and runs the day to day of our little operation."

"That sounds like a good idea," McDonald said.

"I have a new boat coming in the next couple of weeks. Once it arrives, I'll need to go to Nassau to pick it."

"What did you get?" Migos asked.

"AB 100."

"Is it nice?"

"It's the *Sam Houston* on steroids."

"In what way?"

"It's a 100-foot yacht with a max speed of fifty-two knots."

"I didn't think that was possible."

"It is with three V-12 nineteen-hundred-horsepower engines powering waterjets and a space-age composite hull. It also has a two-thousand-mile range. It's going to be awesome."

"What did that run you?" Migos asked.

"A lot, but it's worth it. I learned my lesson from last time. This boat is going to be registered by the CIA through a bunch of different shell companies. It will never be traced to me. It's my last boat."

"You avoided the question."

"Because if I told you, you'd ask me for a raise."

"I already got my raise. I have a ton of un-spendable shiny stuff from the deep parked in a bank vault."

"That's true. I'm surprised none of you guys have turned in your retirement paperwork."

"I'm too young and virile to retire."

"Very true, plus the lifestyle of a swashbuckling, pirate-treasure-hunting mercenary suits you."

"It does. What are you going to name the new boat?"

"Not sure. I'm still working on that."

"We'll brainstorm for you. Help you out. Otherwise, knowing you, it will be the *Sam Houston II*."

"It would be, only that would defeat the whole purpose of having to sink *Sam Houston I*."

"Good, so we're safe on that end. How about 'Pirate Booty'? You get it, it's a pun."

"Don't help with the name Migos; I can do it myself."

The next two weeks were uneventful. The guys settled into a routine of working out, fishing, surfing, and hanging out at the few nightspots on the island. I spent the mornings surfing and then divided my afternoon time between my home office and Trident's headquarters building in Governors Harbour.

Cheryl managed our countersurveillance operation. She stayed in touch with David Forrest and Langley. Cheryl, over the years, had cultivated her own human assets on the island and she worked that surveillance network along with the electronic one provided by David.

Mike made an unannounced visit. Maria brought him up to the top floor of the beach house to my office. I was sitting behind my desk and didn't notice him until the elevator door opened.

"What are you up to?" Mike asked. We shook hands and moved over to the sitting area.

"The team is in hide mode. We're not up to much of anything," I said.

"Keep them alert; the Chinese have definitely figured out it was us that took out their fake islands."

"How do you know?"

"The actions they've taken in response have been uncharacteristically swift."

"I thought they were a patient people, one-hundred-year strategies and all of that."

"That's what we've been taught, but in the last week, they've greenlighted some long-standing attack plans against the USA."

"Like what? I haven't seen anything in the papers."

"You saw the article about the Commander of the 5th Fleet in Bahrain dying?"

"I did. They said it was a heart attack."

"Chemically induced heart attack. Another flag officer, the Deputy Commander of PACOM, an Army Lieutenant General, was in Tripler Hospital getting routine knee surgery and he died from the same thing."

"What happened?"

"An IV he was given during surgery contained a drug cocktail that sent him into a lethal cardiac arrest."

"Did you trace it back to the Chinese?"

"We lost five senior military officers in a single week. Car accidents, heart attacks and one provable murder at PACOM. At the same time, we have a huge cyber hack of DoD, coming at us from North Korea, but we know it's China that really controls that facility."

"Is that all?"

"That's all we know about at this point. By all appearances, it seems the Chinese are executing some of the covert plans they have on the shelf against us."

"It's only natural they would retaliate. We hurt them pretty bad and the military option wouldn't end well for them if they decided to attack us overtly."

"Exactly, so it's economic warfare and black ops."

"So, what brings you to beautiful Eleuthera?"

"We're pretty certain they know it was you who attacked them. So far, they've targeted

DoD and rolled up some agency assets they must've had under suspicion as working for us. You're a very likely target. We think if we throw some sunshine on this covert war the Chinese are waging, we can get them to pull back and allow things to simmer down."

"You want to use Trident as bait to catch them in the act?"

"Exactly. We're going to put all of the members of your team under observation and capture the Chinese when they show."

"I was planning on doing that myself. We have Dave Forrest and Cheryl hard at work and if a Chi-Com sapper makes a run at us, we're armed and ready."

"I had something less kinetic in mind. We want to capture the Chinese agents. We'll use your team as the bait and the team I just landed with will watch and wait. Once the Chinese make their move, we'll capture them."

"Who thinks capturing some Chinese doing a hit on Americans will be enough to cause the Chinese to stop the covert war?"

"I do. Like you said, the Chinese are patient. They're very aggressive when the lights are out, especially when it comes to industrial espionage, but if they earn a reputation for conducting overt attacks in foreign nations, they're going to find fewer countries who will invite them in as trade partners. The long game for them is to achieve hegemony first by starting with trade and finishing with force. Heavy-handed thuggery early on doesn't play to their plan."

"You have confidence in the analysts who come up with this stuff?"

"Yeah, it's what we do. They're not always right but we have to play the odds."

"Your team better be good at staying undetected. Because if one of my guys spots a tail, they're liable to become violent."

"Give your guys a heads-up that another blue team is in the sandbox."

"Ok, but don't you think it would be a good idea to introduce them and maybe share and liaise a bit?"

"Communication with the CIA protection team isn't possible; they're under deep cover."

"Since when is that a problem?"

"Since we're dealing with assets that belong to someone other than me. Not my territory, not my rules."

CHAPTER 12

ELEUTHERA, BAHAMAS

HUANG STEPPED OFF the charter boat and onto the dock in Cotton Bay. The trip from Nassau to the southern tip of Eleuthera Island took five hours. He was still feeling a little bit queasy when he noticed an elderly local man in a straw-hat waving at him. He went to the man and quickly completed a set of rental car paperwork and headed north to Governors Harbour in an old Jeep Cherokee.

The drive to Governors Harbour took over two hours. His motion sickness received little reprieve due to the rough roads which were made even worse by the worn-out shocks in the old Jeep. Huang collapsed onto his bed the moment he reached his room at the French Leave Resort. After a rest, he walked to dinner at the hotel restaurant. The 1648 restaurant was located across Queens Highway, which is a two-lane hardball road bisecting the hotel grounds. Following a light dinner, he set off on foot to find Trident Headquarters. The short walk along Queens Highway into the small downtown area of Governors Harbour was almost all downhill.

He stopped at a picturesque vantage overlooking the town center and spotted the converted mansion Trident used for its headquarters. It was right where he was told it would be, the nearest building to the sea wall on Queens Highway and less than one hundred yards from the small intersection that represented the core of the downtown. The buildings close to the Trident Headquarters included a bank, the police station, two small grocery stores, a liquor store, gas station, bakery, and a real estate office.

Huang continued his walk down the hill to the downtown and sat on a park bench next to the sea wall. He watched as the sun set over the Caribbean in a beautiful spectrum of yellows and blues. At the same time, he kept an eye on the stately two-story stucco mansion across the road. At a little past six, he watched two women exit the building. Both were black Bahamian women who got into separate cars and left. Minutes later, an Asian woman exited the front door and got into a late model Q36 Infinity and drove off.

Late the next morning, Huang drove to a grocery store in downtown Governors Harbour and bought a fishing rod with spinning reel and some bait and tackle. He also picked up a small cooler he filled with bottled water and snacks. He returned to the same bench on the sea wall, slathered himself with sunblock, put a straw hat on his head and began a day of fishing. A few hours later, he watched a late-model blue Chevy Tahoe pull up to the Trident office. Two big men got out of the SUV and entered the house. The man on the driver's side matched the description of his target, at least his height and build did. Huang was more than one hundred yards away and couldn't make out any facial features. With nothing else to go on, he reeled in his line and left his equipment by the bench as if he were going on a quick bathroom break. Huang pulled a small black device the size of a lighter from his pocket and switched it on. The GSM transmitter locator would send a signal every fifteen seconds to the receiving unit in his Jeep. Huang walked across the street and headed directly to the blue Tahoe. When he reached the back of the vehicle, he knelt down to tie his shoe and, using the magnet on the device, he attached it to the rear undercarriage of the Tahoe. He was up in just a few seconds and continued on to the bakery next to the house.

After sitting down and eating a sandwich lunch at Peggy's Bakery, Huang returned back to his park bench and continued to fish. At half-past three, almost four hours after the men arrived, the sweat-soaked Huang saw the two men leave the house, get in their truck and drive up the hill toward the Atlantic side of the island. Huang went to his Jeep and powered up the receiver. He blasted the air conditioning while the system booted up. After a few minutes, his tablet receiver displayed a map with a circular blue icon showing the Tahoe moving south on Banks Road. After a few miles, the vehicle turned into a driveway and stopped. He marked the position on the map and pulled up a Google satellite image of the location. The image showed a main house, two smaller guest houses, and a swimming pool. It was a luxury oceanfront estate on the Atlantic side of the island. On the opposite side of Banks Road was the Leon Levy Native Plant Preserve. The estate had a fence along the rectangular property barrier, except on the side with the beach. On the north side of the property was Tippy's restaurant and on the south side was another deluxe estate.

After studying the map for several minutes, Huang decided to drive by and have a look at the property and the security setup. He didn't slow when he passed the home. It was a three-story stucco structure. The surrounding fence was wrought iron with brick pillars. The gate looked solid, but there was no security personnel.

Huang maintained surveillance of the Trident Headquarters for three days. When he was done fishing each day, he used some of the remaining daylight to scout the beach house. He was pleased about his fishing spot becoming less conspicuous when a couple of other anglers noticed he was having good luck fishing from the park bench and decided to join him. He surreptitiously captured a picture of the men in the Tahoe and from the digital image was able to confirm the presence of his target Pat Walsh. After the third day, he had what he needed and decided it was time to move from surveillance mode to action. That evening, the rest of his team arrived on the ferry from Nassau to Governors Harbour and checked into his hotel.

CHAPTER 13

ELEUTHERA, BAHAMAS

I SAT AT THE head of the dining room table and waited for my lobster bisque to cool. Cheryl had been doing most of the cooking since Maria and her husband had left for vacation. It took a lot of prompting from me to get my loyal housekeeping staff out of harm's way. Father Tellez, my other permanent tenant, couldn't be persuaded to travel. Despite my warnings of the risks, he remained a fixture around the house. All of the other members of the team were assembled around the table.

"After lunch, Savage and I will drive to the Trident office. The rest of you stay inside the house and be ready in case I call for help," I said.

"Stay inside the house. Where have I heard that before?" Cheryl muttered, obviously testy about having been confined inside the house for the better part of a week.

"The Agency has eyes on our fisherman and on the hit team that's staying at the French Leave Resort," I said.

"Is today the day?" Savage asked.

"They think so. I don't think the Chinese would want them hanging around any longer than they have to."

"What's their extraction plan?" McDonald asked.

"I don't know; the agency's keeping me in the dark on a lot of things. I'm getting everything through Mike. It has to be either boat or plane. If it were me, I'd extract out of Governors Harbour Airport in a private jet. Getting out by boat is too slow. Nassau's a fifty-mile boat ride, which is a lot of exposure on the getaway," I said.

"Does the Agency have the airport covered?" Migos asked.

"I don't know. They refuse to communicate or cooperate. Mike doesn't have control in the Caribbean and his counterpart at Langley doesn't want to blow the cover of his agents to civilians."

"We're civilians?" asked Migos.

"All I know is that the Agency picked up the fisherman when he arrived by private boat charter earlier this week and they've been surveilling the hit team since it arrived two nights ago on the ferry."

"And the plan is for you and Savage to just sashay up to the office as bait?" Cheryl asked.

"That's the plan. It's simple enough; they'll take down the Chinese when they make their move. The Agency is calling the shots. We just need to follow the plan, and nothing will go wrong," I said.

"And yet, it so often does," Migos said.

"No, it usually doesn't go wrong. This island is the worst place for a group of Chinese agents to operate. They'll stick out badly. They're either going to plan to kill us as we go in or as we come out. The options are pretty limited," I said.

"They may try a snatch and grab," Cheryl said.

"You used to work with them. Do you think they want a prisoner?" I asked.

"They wouldn't try to take you both. To take one, they would have a team of at least four operators in close, plus a sniper overlooking the target area for observation and security. They'll also have a driver nearby." Cheryl paused, putting her right index finger to her cheek in thought.

"It will be easier to take you going in. If it were me, when you park at the office, you'd be approached simultaneously from both sides. One team would take out Savage with a silenced kill shot. The other would subdue you and then all four would bundle you up and toss you into a vehicle."

"Are you just going to trust the Agency is watching over you?" Migos said between spoonfuls of soup.

"All I know is the Chinese are under Agency surveillance. I expect the Agency to make its move at the same time or just before the Chinese operators. If I pull into that parking space and I see a Chinese person approaching, or better yet two, I'm going to start shooting regardless of what the CIA plan is," I said.

"Me too," said Savage

"And what are we going to be doing again?" Asked Migos.

"Staying inside the house. You're the quick reaction force, except Cheryl. She stays put no matter what," I said.

"I could wear a disguise," said Cheryl.

"Not worth the risk. If they find out you didn't die in Oman, but instead skipped out on them and are working with a CIA-linked company, you're dead. They'll come after you with everything they have."

We finished lunch and Savage and I walked out to the driveway. It was a warm afternoon and the Miguel Caballero level II soft armor undershirt I was wearing under my Tommy Bahama shirt was making me sweat. On my hip, I was sporting an H&K USP 9mm in a rotating hip holster that allowed me to draw quickly even while seated in the truck. Savage and I were both wearing blue-tooth earpieces and throat mics that let us communicate with the rest of the team.

It was almost one in the afternoon when I pulled onto Queens Highway and approached the Trident office. To the right of my usual parking spot was Jessica's car. I didn't recognize the Ford Taurus with heavily tinted windows on the left side of my empty spot.

I pulled forward into the parking space. I unholstered my pistol as I opened the driver's seat door. A man was getting out of the driver's side door on the opposite side of the Taurus as I opened my door. In an instant, the driver's head turned into a red mist. A second later, I heard the report from the sniper shot and then behind me, three rapid weapon discharges. My eyes spent too much time loitering on the head shot victim, and I noticed the open window on the Taurus passenger side too late. I felt the shock of the Taser as I was stepping around my car door. A surge of electricity pouring through my body, dropping me to the ground. My falling down must have cleared the field of fire for a CIA shooter behind me because the Taser gunner was shot through the forehead while he was only a couple seconds into tasering me.

Savage pulled me up by the arm.

"Are you all right?"

"Yeah, I'm fine. Was that it?"

"I think so," he said while looking around. We still hadn't seen any Agency personnel.

"Let's go check on Jessica and the staff," I said while walking a bit unsteadily toward the front door.

"Base, this is Savage," I heard through my earpiece on my way up the stairs.

"Base, this is Savage," he repeated.

Once inside, I ran up to the second floor and found Jessica sitting behind her desk undisturbed.

"Didn't you hear those shots outside?" I asked incredulously.

"What shots?"

"Look out the front window; the police should arrive at any second."

"Base, this is Savage," I heard again through my headpiece.

I closed the tactical app on my phone and called Cheryl on the cell. The call went right to voicemail.

"Let's get back to the house," I said to Savage. Jessica walked by me on her way to the front window of the building to see what I was talking about. The sight of the four dead bodies caused her to gasp.

"What should I tell the police?" she asked.

"Tell them what you saw."

"Should I mention you and Savage?"

"Definitely," I said.

On the way back to the beach house, I drove while Savage tried unsuccessfully to reach Cheryl, Migos, McDonald, and Sorenson on any of the communications. I called Mike on my cell.

"Something's wrong. I can't reach Cheryl or anyone at the house. Do you have eyes on them?"

"Negative."

"There must be a second team," I said.

"Where are you?" Mike asked.

"I just arrived at the house. I'm wheeling through the gate now."

"We captured two Chinese agents and five more were killed in the attempt to get you. That was all of the Chinese agents we were tracking on the island."

"Watch the exits off the island; I'll let you know what I find."

Everything looked normal until I opened the front door of the house. The first thing that greeted us was a dead Chinese agent lying face down on the hardwood floor of the foyer. Savage and I both approached with pistols drawn.

"Migos!" I yelled.

"Up here!" I heard from the second floor.

"Is it clear?"

"Yes."

Savage and I ran up the stairs. We found Migos in the hallway with a trauma pack next to him working on a badly wounded McDonald who was unconscious and bleeding from a chest wound. Savage joined Migos in the effort and started an IV while Migos worked to seal the sucking chest wound.

"Where's Cheryl and Sorenson?" I asked.

"I don't know," Migos said. He was wearing a blood-stained blue t-shirt that was soaked with sweat.

"Take the Tahoe and get him to the clinic," I said.

I raced through the house and the only thing I found were three dead Chinese agents and enough brass and bullet damage to indicate a fierce firefight. I went out the back door toward the beach and found a backpack with an antenna sticking out the top flap. Inside was a GSM jammer that must have been used to kill the cell phones inside the house. I shut the system off.

"Savage, can you hear me?" I asked.

"We're moving him now," he said.

"I went through the house; I found three dead Chinese agents. Now I'm checking the back."

"Roger."

I approached the pool. On each side of the pool is a building. The building on the left is a pool house and a converted chapel. The one on the right is a guest house that has apartments used by the house caretakers and Father Tellez. I circled around the building to the right. When I reached the far side facing the beach I found Father Tellez kneeling over Sorenson. I stood in silence until Father Tellez finished praying.

"Do you know where Cheryl is?" I asked.

"No," he replied.

"What happened?"

"I was in my apartment when I heard the gunfire coming from the house. It was a long fight, lots of shooting. I stayed down on the floor of my room until the firing stopped, then I came outside and found Sorenson. He was badly wounded, shot many times. I couldn't get help. I tried to stop the bleeding, but I couldn't do it alone. I gave him the last rites and he died. I've stayed with him since. My phone isn't working."

"Your phone works now. McDonald is hurt, Savage and Migos are on the way to the hospital clinic with him. I can't find Cheryl."

"I'll help you look. We can't do anything more for this man."

"Was there any shooting inside this building?" I asked.

"No. What about the chapel, did you hear any firing from there?"

"All of the fighting sounded like it came from the main house. I think Sorenson was shot in the main house and then came here and died. If you look back toward the house, you can see the blood trail."

I noticed what Father Tellez was talking about. Sorenson had pursued someone toward the beach. I walked through the line of palm trees onto the beach. I studied the sand looking for signs of a boat landing. As I got closer to the water, I saw the telltale marks of where a rubber boat had been dragged up on the shore.

"It looks like they came in two Zodiacs."

I called Mike on my cell. I used the encrypted app.

"A Chinese hit team attacked the beach house. Cheryl is missing, Sorenson is dead, and McDonald is badly wounded and on his way to the clinic in town. He's going to need to be airlifted to Nassau," I said.

"What about Cheryl?"

"The team left in two Zodiacs. We need to find where they went."

"They haven't had enough time to reach the big island. They're either still out on the water or they landed somewhere close on Eleuthera."

"I need direct communication with whoever is in charge of the Agency personnel on the island."

"I'll try to make that happen."

"It was a mistake not to have it to start with."

"Agreed, it was a security protocol. We'll put everything we have into finding her."

I called David Forrest.

"Dave, I need your help."

"What is it?"

"Cheryl's been kidnapped. They took her about half an hour ago from the beach house. They came and left in rubber boats. We need to track all of the boats in the local waters in case they linked up with a mother ship. I think they landed the rubber boats somewhere else on the island and changed transportation or are planning on laying low until they can escape. It's too easy to track the boat traffic."

"What should I search for?"

"They would need a house with privacy. Can you search the vacation rentals and see what you can find? The rental couldn't have been booked before we arrived in Eleuthera unless they killed the occupants; most people book vacation homes months in advance. We need a place where you can put two Zodiacs into the water and take them out without detection from a nosy neighbor."

"I'm sure Langley will support with anything I request. I'll get back to you once I find something."

CHAPTER 14

ELEUTHERA, BAHAMAS

H UANG JUMPED OUT of the Zodiac with the other men and helped pull the heavy rubber boat across the sandy beach and into the storage area under the house. As hurricane protection, the beach house was built on eight-foot stilts which allowed for a perfect space to hide two fifteen-foot rubber boats from aerial observation. Huang led the way into the house through the back deck while two of his men carried the prisoner. The remaining six men finished stowing the two boats and took up security positions around the house.

Huang was soon walking in circles around the island in the center of the kitchen, the pacing helped him contain his anxiety. He frequently checked the settings on his radio, but he was unwilling to use it for fear of giving away his position. As per the plan, the team had gone into silent mode once they began their exfiltration from the objective.

Huang wondered about the fate of the team that had gone after Pat Walsh. He lost contact with the other team very early into the operation. As soon as the tracker he had placed on Pat Walsh's truck indicated movement to the Trident Headquarters, he launched with the boat team. During the infiltration to Walsh's beach house, he was able to monitor the actions of the other team on the radio. The last update he received had them taking position outside of the Trident Headquarters building. After that, the assault on the beach house had consumed all of his attention. It wasn't until the exfiltration began and he was forced into radio silence that he realized he hadn't received an update from the other team since the assault began. Now he had no idea if their mission was successful.

Huang accompanied the boat team because that was the main effort. Capturing Pat Walsh was secondary. The priorities changed after facial recognition software identified the photo of a woman inside the house as a former Chinese Intelligence officer. Having triumphed over the Navy in the tsunami investigation, Huang's boss, the Minister of State Security, now saw an opportunity to earn even more favor with the President at the expense of his rival at the People's Liberation Army. The boat team was originally positioned offshore in a cargo vessel as a contingency force. When knowledge of the female Chinese defector became known, the contingency force was activated and ordered to land in Eleuthera and plan a mission to capture the woman on the fly.

The unconscious woman lying on the living room floor had defected from a highly classified People's Liberation Army Intelligence Agency known as Unit 83461. Unit 83461, referred to in the West simply as Chinese Intelligence, is part of the People's Liberation Army and is the equivalent of the US CIA. It competes with the Ministry of State Security in only a few narrow areas. The MSS is much bigger and has a much broader mission than Unit 83461. MSS has over one hundred thousand employees. MSS agents are embedded in every Chinese technology company and in most foreign hi-tech firms with R&D departments that are doing work worthy enough of being robbed.

Unlike Unit 83461, which was formed by President Mao in the 1940s, MSS wasn't created until 1983. MSS rose to prominence in the 1990s when China decided to open its borders and compete with the world economically. A key part of that economic growth strategically included the theft of technology from the West and from Japan. Industrial espionage remains the sole province of MSS, but in some of the other more traditional intelligence functions, the two agencies share similar responsibilities. The overlapping functions between MSS and Chinese Intelligence are a constant source of friction and the principal reason for the rivalry between the Minister of State Security and the Commander of the People's Liberation Army. The tsunami investigation is a perfect example of how the Chinese President sometimes pits the two agencies against each other. The work of Huang had been a major boon to MSS, and the Minister saw an opportunity to disclose a previously unreported Chinese Intelligence agent defection as an even bigger opportunity to embarrass his PLA rival.

The discovery of the woman was almost by accident. As soon as Pat Walsh was identified as the owner of the *Sam Houston* and it was learned he had a home in Eleuthera, MSS turned on all of its vast resources and went to work dissecting his life. The Bahamian cellphone system is a ZTE network manufactured by the Chinese telecom company

Huawei. Huawei is a very valuable intelligence gathering asset of MSS because it allows the Chinese government to eavesdrop on every phone call and data transmission that goes over the cellphone network. Because all Bahamian customs and passport control data flow through the Huawei cellphone system, it was not difficult for MSS to hack into the immigration database and identify Pat Walsh's travel companions. The name of the person who traveled to the Bahamas most often with Pat Walsh, including on this latest trip, was a woman with a US Passport under the name of Cheryl Li. When the background of Cheryl Li was discovered to be thin, MSS ran a facial recognition using the passport photo in the file. Facial recognition identified the woman as a former Chinese Intelligence agent named Shu Xue Wong. The discovery quickly found its way to the Minister.

Shu Xue Wong had reportedly been killed in a hotel fire in Oman two years earlier. The fire left few survivors and Shu Xue Wong's body was reported as one of dozens of unidentifiable remains. When the Minister learned that the destruction of the Naval bases in the South China Sea was executed by a People's Liberation Army intelligence agent working with the CIA, he immediately elevated Shu Xue Wong to the primary target. News of the PLA's incompetence would finish the MSS rivalry with the PLA. Having lived in the shadow of the PLA for most of his career, the day he presented Shu Xue Wong to President Ping along with a full confession of her treachery would be the best day of the Minister's long and distinguished career. Huang was certain to be rewarded immensely by the grateful Minister.

After a full hour of waiting for contact, Huang finally

resigned himself to the fact that the team he sent to capture Pat Walsh had been killed. He walked over to the kitchen counter and checked the location of Walsh's truck on the tablet tracking system and saw that the truck had moved from the Trident headquarters to a nearby medical clinic. Maybe Walsh was hurt or, better yet, killed in the attack, he thought.

Huang considered his options. He could reinstate the surveillance plan and confirm that Pat Walsh was still alive, and if Walsh was alive, he could mount another attack. He had already lost four men in the capture of Cheryl Li, plus another seven men in the failed attempt to capture Pat Walsh. Law enforcement would be converging on the island, and making another attempt on Walsh while safeguarding his prize would stretch his resources. After several more minutes of pacing and weighing the risks, Huang decided to abandon Walsh and concentrate on getting the traitor off the island and on her way back to China. Later, he would put the boats back into the water and link up with the mother ship that would be in position twelve miles offshore in international waters at midnight.

CHAPTER 15

ELEUTHERA, BAHAMAS

P ETER HAWES WAS a short, wiry, blond-haired man who sported retro John Lennon glasses. Pat guessed the CIA Station Chief was in his late thirties. He was accompanied by another agent, a slightly overweight black man, whose hair was going to grey and who spoke hardly at all. The two CIA agents brought with them five heavily-armed soldiers who Pat assumed were SAD operators. CIA Special Activities Division recruited from USSOCOM and they performed most of the paramilitary jobs required by the Agency. The five men all had the telltale physiques and demeanors of top-level special operators, which is why he assumed they were SAD.

Peter Hawes, Pat, Savage, and Migos sat at the kitchen table while the SAD operators stood away from the table, leaning against the cabinets. The bodies of Chinese operators had been removed by a CIA cleanup team and the damaged house was eerily silent.

"What are you doing to find Cheryl?" Pat asked.

"We're watching the airports and ferry landings."

"How did they land a second team without you knowing?"

"I don't know. We picked up one team that landed by private boat charter from Nassau. We have no idea how the second team got in."

"Did you have anyone watching the house during the op?"

"No, we were too thin; we had all of our assets surrounding the Trident Headquarters. We figured your guys could take care of themselves."

"They attacked the house with at least ten people; they wouldn't have used two boats for less. They killed Sorenson and wounded McDonald. The Chinese had four killed; we don't know how many—if any—were wounded, but I think we're looking for up to seven Chinese and one prisoner."

"The rubber boats and the equipment mean they didn't come in posing as tourists. Rubber boats don't have much range and can't handle tough seas. They must have been dropped offshore by a larger vessel. Most likely that's also going to be their way out."

"We've had ISR covering the waters around the target area ever since the attack. There has been no linkup between rubber boats and a mother ship."

"Which means Cheryl is still on the island."

"We think so. The boats must have landed nearby, and the Chinese must be hiding somewhere on the island. We would've found the boats if they were still on the water twenty minutes after the attack."

"We need to search every house on the Atlantic side of this island to the north and south of this house for at least ten miles in each direction."

"How many houses is that?"

"Thirty, maybe forty houses."

"Let's split up and walk the beach. We'll put everyone on the same comms for once. We can keep a small QRF here with a vehicle."

I stayed with Peter and two of his operators while Migos and Savage and the rest of the agency personnel walked the beach. It was late in the afternoon and we only had a few hours of remaining light. I checked in with Mike and gave him an update. I told him I wasn't all that impressed with Peter Hawes. He didn't seem to know him, but I could tell he was frustrated with the communications he had with his counterpart, who was the man that Hawes reported to.

The teams kept us up to date on their progress as they walked the beach line and searched for signs of the Chinese rubber boats. It was getting dark and the teams had only covered a third of the territory the boats could have used to beach. I was growing more and more despondent by the minute as the hope of finding Cheryl seeped from my soul.

David Forrest called as the sun was setting.

"I have a house I think you should check."

"Is it a last-minute rental?"

"No, it was booked many months ago."

"Why did you flag it?" I asked.

"It's located four miles due South of your house. It's in a cove with a very private beach. The booking was made by a New Jersey college professor named Neil Sullivan. I tried to call the cell number on the booking, and it went to voicemail. I tracked down his daughter and found out a few things. The Sullivans and their close friends, another older couple named the Krantzbergs, rented the house six days ago for two weeks. Nobody has been able to contact either couple the past three days. Sullivan's daughter was worried and was getting ready to notify the authorities when I reached her."

"What's the address on the booking?"

"It's the Kataluma House on Palmetto Point."

"Do you have ISR over it?"

"Not yet. I will in another twenty minutes."

"Keep me updated."

Peter had been sitting across the kitchen table eaves-dropping on the conversation with Dave.

"What do you have?"

"Kataluma House on Palmetto Point. It's in a big cove, four miles due south from here. Your guys are closest. Have them set up surveillance."

"Just to be clear, this is my operation. I'm going to lead with my own personnel; your guys are going to be in reserve," Hawes said.

"That's fine. Let's get a team with eyes on the house and then move everyone else into position in case we have to go in."

I rode with Hawes and his team in his GMC Yukon. We pulled off Queens Highway about one hundred yards from a private road that led to the house. It was dark by the time we hid the truck inside the wood-line. I called David Forrest. He had a Predator UAV feed, but all it showed was the house and two cars. The Chinese, if there were any Chinese, were all under cover.

One of Hawes's operators met us at the truck. I was glad they were with us. Although I never saw any of the SAD operators during the skirmish at the Trident Headquarters,

I saw how efficiently they dispatched the Chinese agents, and I was comfortable with their skills.

The operator was in the same beachwear he had been sporting to walk the beach on the earlier reconnaissance. It was dark and the bugs were in full bloom. The SAD operator and his partner had crawled to the edge of the woods to scout the house armed only with pistols.

"The house is on stilts. Underneath at the corners they've positioned operators with rifles. There's also one machine gun. From the wood-line to the house is a hundred yards of flat open lawn. They have night vision. There's no way to get to the house unobserved."

"What about from the beach?"

"Same thing. It's flat open ground from the water. They'll see you coming in."

"What do you suggest we do?"

"We watch and wait. We have ISR above; we'll cover the road going out and the route to the beach if they try to escape on the water."

"We wait until they try to move her and make our move then?"

"Yes, it's too dangerous to assault the house; they'll kill her before we ever get close."

Hawes was making a lot of sense. I sat in the SUV watching and listening to the internal radio traffic as Hawes positioned the teams onto vantage points where they could cover the exits from the house. By the time Migos and Savage arrived, the SAD operators had all switched into full tactical gear with body armor, night vision, and helmets. The three of us were the reserve force; we stayed five hundred yards from the house in the vehicle parked just inside the wood-line off of Queens Highway. We waited for several hours before anything happened. At eleven, David Forrest called me and alerted us that four men were carrying a rubber boat to the water. I passed the message to Hawes and the rest of the team over the radio. One of the SAD teams confirmed they had eyes on the movement. Hawes had placed a two-man sniper position overlooking the beach. I had seen what his snipers could do earlier in the day and was positive that boat would never leave the beach.

"I have three people moving from the house to the beach. Two tangoes are carrying the package," I heard the SAD team with the callsign Hotel say over the open net.

Hawes had two personnel blocking the road from the house to Queens Highway. He had a two-man team overlooking the house and another two-man team closer to the shoreline overlooking the beach. He called the beach team Bravo, the house team Hotel, and the road team Romeo. Savage, Migos, and I began to slowly walk toward the house. If we were needed, we didn't want to have to cover the full five hundred yards.

"Hotel, do you have a shot on the tangoes carrying the package?" I heard Hawes say over the radio.

"Affirmative."

"Hotel and Bravo team, engage."

The woods in front of us erupted in gunfire. As we walked toward the sound of the gunfire from the team covering the house, I could imagine the firefight to our front. It was essential the first shots killed the men carrying Cheryl to the boat. The snapping of rounds clipping the trees around us was our first indication of return fire. A louder, staccato burst of a machine gun drowned out all of the other gunfire. We hit the deck as orange tracers cut down the trees all around us.

I high crawled as fast as I could on my knees and elbows toward the edge of the tree line so I could see what was going on. Unlike the SAD operators, I didn't have any tactical gear or night vision. My knees and elbows were a bloody mess by the time I reached the edge of the woods. The machine gun was still firing when I reached the open area. I could no longer hear any return fire from either of the SAD teams. I found a small earthen mound and began to pump rounds at the muzzle flash of the machine gun located at the rear corner of the house. Migos plopped down in the prone five yards to my left and opened fire. I was wondering where Savage was when I heard him over the radio.

"Cover me, I'm flanking on your right."

"Changing mag!" I heard Migos yell. I continued to fire until machine gun bullets crawled up the mound I was using for protection. I ducked for cover while dirt and rocks fell all around me.

"Changing mag!" I yelled as I slapped in my third and last magazine. Migos picked up the firing.

"Lift fire!" I heard Savage yell over the net. I rolled to my right, jumped up and raced toward the house. Savage was a shadow seventy-five yards in front of me. He ran at a full sprint towards the firing machine gun that was concentrating on Migos. Savage shot and killed the man behind the machine gun and continued to race toward the beach without breaking stride. I followed Savage, but he moved like a deer and I couldn't keep up.

We ran toward a cluster of people on the ground in the open lawn. One man raised a pistol and fired at the charging Savage. He missed. Savage, still in a sprint, shot the man twice and slid to his knees on the wet grass to a small prostrate body. I watched Savage touch the side of her neck in search of a pulse. I reached the cluster of bodies seconds behind Savage. Cheryl was lying face down on the grass. I put my hand on the back of her head and felt warm blood. I turned her limp body onto her back and tried to resuscitate her with breaths of air. She wasn't breathing and there was no pulse. I cleared the airway again and gave her two strong breaths. Then I compressed her chest and repeated. I don't know how long I tried, but eventually, Migos stopped me by putting his hand on my chest.

Migos sat next to me on the wet grass. My face and hands were sticky with Cheryl's blood. My arms were around my knees and my head was buried in my forearms. I had a ton of regrets. Taking Cheryl to Eleuthera had been monumentally stupid, not expecting an attack on the beach house even more so. Letting the CIA's obsession with security trump reasonable operations requirements to share communications was even dumber still. In a single day I got Cheryl killed, Sorenson killed, and McDonald was in Nassau fighting for his life. I was finding it difficult to breathe.

Eventually, I pulled my head up and surveyed the lawn in the moonlight. Next to Cheryl were the bodies of two Chinese agents. The Chinese were dressed in tactical gear and had died with weapons slung because their hands were occupied with carrying Cheryl. One of the two had drawn a pistol and shot at Savage. I grabbed his pistol and dropped the mag. I pressed it and found only one round had been expended. The other Chinese agent carrying Cheryl had died from the initial sniper volley.

Looking toward the house, I could see the silhouette of the machine gunner and his ammo bearer behind a support column. Both were lying on their backs where Savage had dispatched them. Cheryl wasn't hit by a 7.62 machine gun round; the head wound would be much bigger than it was. I could tell that much. If the two agents carrying her didn't kill her and the machine gun didn't get her, then who did?

Farther down toward the beach, I could see a rubber boat at the edge of the sand and a few lumps that must have been the boat team. Two SAD operators were searching the bodies. It wasn't very likely someone from the boat team was able to shoot Cheryl.

"What's the original headcount on the tangoes?" I asked over my radio.

"Seven," I heard Hawes say. He was inside the house with two other agents conducting a search.

"Did one of them get away?" I asked

"Let me check."

I called David Forrest.

"Did you see a tango squirt south on the predator feed?" I asked.

"I have one track. I thought it was a friendly."

"Where is he now?"

"In the woods, stationary, about two hundred yards south of the house."

"I'm moving with Migos and Savage; vector us to the target."

"ISR has a fix; Migos and Savage on me," I said as I began to walk south. The crashing surf to our left masked our movement as the three of us left the open lawn and stepped into the woods. None of us were wearing night vision goggles or had any ballistic protection. We were in casual clothing carrying M4 carbines at the ready.

"Seventy-five meters south," I heard David say over my phone.

The three of us formed a line, ten yards between us as we slowly walked through the pine forest.

"Seventy-five yards, due south," I said into my radio microphone.

"Fifty yards, same azimuth," I heard David say a minute later.

"Fifty yards," I repeated for Migos and Savage to hear.

We slowed our advance. The forest thinned, allowing more moonlight to filter through. To the east, we could see the white bioluminescent surf. The sounds of crickets and surf filled my ears as we crept steadily on.

"Twenty-five yards. He's in a prone position behind a tree directly in front of you," I heard David say.

With my right thumb, I moved the selector switch on my carbine from semi to auto and pulled the trigger as I sprinted forward. I barely registered the muzzle flashes to my direct front. It took only three seconds to close the distance. In my hands, I felt the bolt of my carbine lock back when the magazine emptied. I pounced on the figure lying on his belly, I brought the buttstock of my weapon down as hard as I could bring it at his head. The man had cat-like reflexes. He rolled quickly to his right and evaded the blow. I snapped the collapsible buttstock in half when the weapon hit the ground. I dropped the weapon and fell onto the man. I drove my right elbow into his face as he tried to raise a pistol with his right hand. I grabbed his right wrist with my left hand, pivoted around and drove punch after punch into his face. A shoulder wound prevented him from moving his left arm. He dropped the pistol moments before he lost consciousness. I hit him another twenty or thirty times before my right hand grew numb and the fatigue slowed me down.

Savage and Migos walked up next to me while I was still sitting on the Chinese agent's chest.

"Is he dead?" Migos asked.

I placed the index and forefinger of my left hand on the man's bloody neck.

"No, not yet anyway," I said.

"What was that all about?" Savage asked.

"This guy killed Cheryl," I said as I stood up.

"Are you sure?" Savage asked.

"Yes, I'm sure."

Migos stepped in and delivered a wicked kick into the man's side; the snap of his ribcage was loud enough to be heard back at the house.

"Let's get him back to the house and turn him over to our overlords," I said.

"Those guys are pros; what's your beef with them?"

"The SAD operators are excellent; its prep school Pete from Broughton and Yale I could live without," I said.

"You blame him for Cheryl's death?"

"No, I just don't like the guy," I said.

CHAPTER 16

ELEUTHERA, BAHAMAS

FATHER TELLEZ CELEBRATED Cheryl's funeral in the tiny chapel behind the beach house. The Catholic Church would likely punish the good Father if they discovered he was using the Catholic rites to send off a Buddhist, but that kind of thing never seemed to bother Father Tellez. The Chapel only seats twenty-eight. With groups from Trident, Clearwater, and the Agency it was standing room only.

Mike showed up as the service was beginning. We didn't have a chance to talk until much later when everyone was up at the house eating lunch. I was sitting on the porch, staring out at the ocean, nursing a Scotch when he found me.

"How are you holding up?"

"Good."

"You blame yourself, don't you?"

"Disaster follows me wherever I go, so I've become pretty good at understanding it."

"What does that mean?"

"It's never a single mistake—it's always a chain of errors. Staying too long over the demo site because we wanted to remove the treasure, returning back here instead of going to a CIA safe house, failing to pick up the second team of Chinese, not having direct commo with the Agency people involved in the operation. This was just an unforgivable cluster fuck of epic proportions."

"It was, but it's not all on you."

"I'm not looking for absolution. I screwed up, people died. It's not the first time; I've been running teams for thirty years. It's time to step away from it all and leave this kind of work to younger, sharper, more focused minds."

"You didn't kill Sorenson and you didn't kill Cheryl; that was done by MSS."

"How do you know that?"

"That Chinese agent you beat the crap out of is singing. Even with a badly broken face and a jaw that's held together by wire."

"What's going to happen to him?"

"He's going to eventually be swapped along with the other two minions we caught in this operation. Until then we'll continue to interrogate him."

"Was he the one who killed Cheryl?"

"Yeah."

"He didn't need to do that. He was beaten and he executed her, just so we couldn't have her."

"That's exactly what he did."

"We should've kept Cheryl under lock and key."

"She never would've allowed it. You act you like you ever had control over the woman. It was always the other way around and you know it."

"It was. I don't think I ever said no to her."

"You didn't. She escaped from the Chinese regime and she died a free woman. Leave it at that."

We sat in peace for several minutes, watching the Atlantic swells over the tree line from the high deck. I nursed my Scotch. It tasted bitter, much like the world at the moment.

"Go pick up that new boat you ordered. I'm coming back in a few weeks and I'm going to give you a chance at payback."

"When did China become your problem? Are you no longer just the Middle East?"

"I'm the guy who freed the South China Sea from the grip of the Chinese Dragon. You're talking to the new Chief of Clandestine Ops."

"That's a win for the good guys."

"We have lots more to do, Pat. Go pick up your new boat. Decompress; I'll be in touch soon. Getting back in the field is the best way to take your mind off your loss," Mike said as he gave me a hug and then walked away.

The next few days were a blur. Savage, Migos, and I traveled to Wisconsin to attend Sorenson's funeral. Almost everyone from my old unit is divorced. Guys like Sorenson— even though they only served twelve years—would have spent almost all of that time deployed in direct combat. It's a lifestyle that's not easy on a family, especially with the obsessive secrecy the unit imposes where you can't share anything with anyone who is not in the unit.

I met Sorenson's parents, his two sisters, his ex-wife, and his two young children. Unlike Cheryl's service, the Sorenson funeral packed a five-thousand-seat church in the small town where they all lived in rural Wisconsin. Shrek was an immensely popular guy who, as I learned, was also a brilliant student-athlete in high school and college. He played football for Notre Dame and after graduation enlisted in the Army on an Airborne Ranger contract. He made Staff Sergeant in the 1st Ranger Battalion in only five years. The Rangers conduct a lot of missions with CAG and when the unit guys identify a Ranger leader with sufficient talent, they direct the person to try out for the varsity squad. Sorenson left the JV (Rangers) and went on to serve another seven years with the varsity at Fort Bragg before separating from the Army as a Sergeant First Class. The CIA recruited him out of CAG and placed him with Trident.

At Trident, we require everyone to have an updated will, which made the lawyers' task of carving up Sorenson's estate that much easier. Savage was able to recover Sorenson's pirate bounty from the bank in Grand Cayman and we turned it over to a reputable law firm and a solid international coin dealer to liquidate and disperse with the estate. We no longer had to worry about the Chinese using it as a clue to find us. The Sorenson family were solid Midwesterners and they didn't seem all that impressed with their newfound wealth. I stuck around for two days. I didn't think it was possible to feel worse than I already did, but when I met Sorenson's family, I discovered a new depth of sadness. I began to see the pirate treasure as a curse.

CHAPTER 17

NASSAU, BAHAMAS

MIKE CALLED ME earlier in the day to let me know that the boat was ready for pickup. The Agency handled the paperwork, making sure the purchase would never be traced to me or Trident. When I arrived at the marina, I gave the gate guard an alias ID and he let me through. I spotted the white yacht with the distinctive black hull as I stepped through the gate. In a marina filled with beautiful yachts, the AB 100 stood out. The sleek, hundred-foot yacht was docked at the farthest slipway from the entrance. As I approached, for the first time in weeks my spirits lifted, and I became excited. The profile of the boat exudes speed; it looks like a cigarette boat with three decks. The yacht is magnificent.

I found the keys where Mike said they would be, hidden in a chair next to the garage by the hydraulic ramp at the tail of the stern. I opened the garage, which was twice the size of the one on my old boat and found a thirteen-foot tender and a jet ski. A curved staircase flanked both sides of the garage. I went up the starboard side to the main deck.

I unlocked the triple glass doors and went into the salon. The interior was white, with a beige carpet. A sixty-inch TV was mounted against the wall to the right of the entrance. Facing the TV was a modular set of two grey couches and two grey chairs arrayed in a horseshoe with a coffee table in the center. Farther in, the carpet turned to blonde wood and I moved past the living room to a dining area and then to the wheelhouse. The interior was bright, the walls of the main deck held large rectangular glass windows, and the wheelhouse cockpit had a huge windshield. Inside the wheelhouse were two big captain's chairs and three impressive 42-inch monitors to display the ship's controls. A small black steering wheel was mounted in front of the central monitor along with the thrust controls for the three V-12 1800 HP MAN engines and generator systems. The modern space-age design of the wheelhouse made it possible by camera to have a 360-degree view of the entire yacht.

Between the dining area and the wheelhouse, I took the spiral staircase down to the lower deck. The walls and floors of the lower deck were the same clean blond hardwood as found on the main deck. In the center of the deck, I found the owner's cabin and behind the owner's cabin was the engine room. Forward of the owner's cabin were the remainder of the staterooms and the galley. The owner's cabin is the full twenty-two feet width of the boat. It's a spacious living space with a king bed and a large modern bathroom plus a seating area and walk-in closet. All four bedrooms were carpeted with large picture windows. The galley was a long, narrow, stainless-steel professional kitchen with a small breakfast nook attached. I then took the stairs up to the flydeck, the place on the *Sam Houston* where I spent most of my time. The flydeck was huge— twice the size of the one on the *Sam Houston*. The flydeck had its own helm station to pilot the yacht, a king-sized sunbathing bed, and two couches wrapped around a stainless-steel table. It also had a bar, a fridge, and a well-equipped gas grill. Looking down from the helm station, I could see the bow of the yacht which had another sunbathing bed connected to a circular lounging area with a table in the center.

I spent a few hours studying the technical manuals of the engines, generators, navigation, stabilization, and jet propulsion systems. It wasn't until just before five in the afternoon that I took the boat out from the Nassau Marina. The trip to Runaway Cove Marina in Governors Harbour, Eleuthera, took just over an hour. The yacht has a cruising speed of forty knots, and I couldn't resist testing it at one point and getting it up to its full speed of fifty-four knots which was two knots faster than advertised. Squeezing the big boat into the tiny marina was very difficult; I had only two feet on either side of the yacht as I threaded the needle through the narrow marina entrance on the Caribbean side. The task was made much easier with the stitched 360-degree external camera system, warning sensors, and the side jets that allowed the yacht to move in any direction with great precision.

I spent the next two days provisioning the yacht for the trip to Cyprus. The work was the perfect distraction from the thoughts and memories that had been haunting me for the past weeks. I still hadn't named the boat the evening before I set sail for the Mediterranean. I considered and discarded hundreds of options and couldn't find one I liked. The ones I liked—like *Susu, Cheryl, Rising Sea*, and *Sam*

Houston II— defeated my goal of anonymous ownership. I was at the kitchen table reviewing the weather report on my laptop when Maria came in carrying a big package.

"What's that?" I asked.

"It was delivered by courier for you this afternoon. It doesn't say who sent it," she said as she lifted the big package that was an inch thick and had dimensions of 4 x 1 foot.

"Let's open it."

Maria cut the paper wrapping off revealing a white signboard with black trim underneath. She tilted the sign so I could see it better. It read *Wayward Nomad.*

"What is it?" Maria asked.

"I think the CIA has named my new boat for me," I said.

"Do you like it?"

"Not especially, but I don't disagree with the description. It'll work."

"Do you want me to have Jonah put it on?" she asked.

"Yes, thanks. Make sure he knows the hull's composite. I don't think you can screw the name on—he might have to glue it."

"He'll figure it out."

CHAPTER 18

ATLANTIC OCEAN

THE FIRST LEG of the journey was due east from the Bahamas to the Canary Islands, which are west of Africa. The journey is two thousand miles, which is the maximum range of the *Nomad* and I expected it to take a little over a week. The *Wayward Nomad* was built in Italy, but it made its first transatlantic crossing as cargo; this would be its first real sea trial and I was excited to learn how to handle the yacht and see how it would perform. Although the yacht has a cruising speed of forty knots, to conserve fuel I was planning to make the crossing at twenty-one knots.

Father Tellez drove to the marina with me early in the morning to see me off and return my truck to the house. He gave the yacht a blessing. My first task was to check how Jonah had mounted the name above the garage door at the stern of the boat; it looked good.

"Why this name?" Father Tellez said with a disapproving look, pointing at the nameboard.

"The Chinese tracked us down and killed Cheryl by tracing the *Sam Houston* to me. The CIA bought this one through a bunch of shell companies to hide my ownership. They're the ones who named it. It was probably Mike who chose the name."

"This is not a name to aspire to," he said.

"No, I don't think it is."

"You should change it."

"I'm going to leave it for now."

"It's a very showy boat. I don't think it's practical for your work."

"I'm not a spy; I never was. I don't like the clandestine stuff. I never have."

"You work for the CIA. The Agency bought your boat to hide your ownership. How does that not make you a spy?"

"It's a complicated world. All I know is that I like to travel, and I like to live on a boat, and this is a really great boat. The contract work Trident does is mostly logistics and where I live and how I live has nothing to do with the job."

"Mostly logistics, but it's not the logistics that you need to worry about."

"Come on up. Let's have a cup of coffee on the flydeck before I depart. It's a beautiful morning."

The tiny fishing fleet from the marina had already departed for the day. The marina manager is an elderly Bahama native, a rail-thin black man named Bill. He's a master mechanic who's always looked after my boat when it's in the Bahamas. He notified me that he checked everything out and filled the water and fuel and we were ready to go.

Father Tellez chose a couple of K-cups and we brewed two cups of very good coffee before we walked up the stairs to the roofless flydeck. We sat at the table on separate couches looking out at the turquoise waters of the Caribbean. It was a typical winter morning in Eleuthera, the weather was eighty-one degrees, the water was glassy calm, birds were circling around, and there were only a few clouds in the sky with a warm gentle breeze coming in from the south.

"When will you come back?"

"I don't know; probably not for a few months."

"Where are you going?"

"Cyprus."

"Then where?"

"I don't know where to after that."

"Why don't you know?"

"I just don't."

"Could you tell me if you did?"

"No, I don't think I could."

"Why do you do this work, Pat? You don't need the money."

"Every time I try to quit, something brings me back."

"That's not a very good reason."

"I like to have a higher purpose. A reason to get up in the morning."

"Do you ever wonder if you have an addiction to danger?"

"No, I think I have a healthy fear of danger."

"Yet you do very dangerous things."

"Not very often."

"Compared to normal people, it is more than very often."

"What do you recommend?"

"Maybe you should see someone. A professional."

"I get shrinked by an Agency psychiatrist once a year."

"You do?"

"Yes, I do. For the work I do, I'm apparently the epitome of mental hygiene."

"There is nothing normal about any part of your life."

"I know. It's part tragedy and part comedy, but I can't exactly unwind the film."

"You can change the direction you're heading."

"I run a small company that does work for the US Government. I know it's corny, but I believe in what we're doing. I have employees and associates like Mike that count on me and I have other obligations like the foundation that you manage. If I gave everything up, what would I do that would be as worth doing?"

"I've known you for a long time. The wind seems to be gone from your sails. No offense, but you seem to be going through the motions. I don't know much about the work you do, but I know it's far more dangerous than you let on. Staying alive must require someone who is doing more than just going through the motions."

"I'm grieving in my own strange way. I'm hoping that a few weeks at sea, alone, will make me feel better than I feel right now. My plan is that when it's time to get back to work, I won't be on autopilot anymore."

"Then you admit I'm right."

"Of course, you're always right about such things."

"How do you feel right now?"

"Guilty. Very guilty and very sad."

We were silent for a couple of minutes while we drank our coffee and watched the birds dive into the water for their breakfast.

Father Tellez reached over and grabbed my arm.

"We should pray," he said.

CHAPTER 19

ABU DHABI

I WAS ON THE flydeck of the *Wayward Nomad* reading a book on my iPad. I was lying on the couch facing toward the open Arabian Gulf. Off to my left was the enormous Presidential Palace and to my right the equally massive Emirates Palace Hotel. My boat was docked in the Emirates Palace Marina. The sleek one-hundred-foot *Nomad* wasn't the most impressive yacht in the marina by a long shot.

The Emirates Palace Marina is home to more than a hundred boats ranging in size from twenty to two hundred fifty feet. I had used the marina in the past when I had the *Sam Houston*, but I preferred the Intercontinental Marina because it's a much more casual and relaxing place than the Emirates Palace Hotel which has a lot of pretenses. The biggest difference between the Palace and the Intercon were the live-aboards. The boats in the Intercon were much smaller and were used mostly for weekend recreational boating. The Emirates Palace had a lot of those as well, but it also had its share of billionaires' big boats and a fairly large community of expats who lived full time in their boats. Rents in Abu Dhabi rival London, New York, and Tokyo for the most expensive in the world. Rather than paying rent, a lot of western expats use their sizable housing allowance to buy boats to live in. The unusual circumstances of the Abu Dhabi housing market create a very unique situation. Abu Dhabi is possibly the only place in the world where buying a boat can actually be a pretty good investment.

I've been living in the Palace Marina for a month, waiting for instructions from Mike. I stopped in Paphos along the route and uploaded the equipment I'd taken off the *Sam Houston*. I also used the opportunity to covertly arm the boat and cache emergency funds and documents. I took a room in the hotel next door so I could use the gym and the pool. The restaurants at the Emirates Palace are all very good, my two favorites being the outdoor BBQ and the Chinese. The hotel also has a very nice cigar bar. I spent my days waiting for the assignment going to the gym and puttering around the boat. At night I would go to dinner at the hotel and then often find myself on one of my neighbor's boats. The after-dinner cocktail party rotated nightly from boat to boat. Initially, I rebuffed the invitations, but after three refusals, I realized my fellow live-aboards weren't going to relent. My reticence to socialize was inviting more scrutiny than attendance and so, in yet another act of sacrifice for my country, I now find myself on the cocktail circuit—most nights, drinking late into the evening with my fellow mariners.

"Permission to come aboard?" I heard a voice yell from behind me. I turned around and found Mike standing at the side gate. I waved him in. I got up and met Mike on the stairs. We embraced.

"Let's talk in the salon. Not much privacy here in Stepford," I said while looking around, checking for the peering eyes of my nosy neighbors.

"Can I get you a drink?" I asked. Mike walked over to the bar with me and then opened the door to the wine cooler and, without checking, pulled out a bottle of red.

"This will do," he said.

"Aren't you even going to read the label?" I asked.

"If it's in here, I'm sure it's good and that I can't afford it."

I took the bottle from him to open it. It was an Italian, a Sassicaia 2010. It was a good choice.

"You could've given me some warning," I said.

"I thought I would surprise you."

"You're looking fit and tanned," he said.

"I crossed the Atlantic, Mediterranean, and Red Sea. That's a lot of time outside and I'm not that great of a cook."

"How are you feeling?"

"I'm good. Ready to get back to work."

"The life of leisure with the rest of the boat people isn't doing it for you?"

"It gets boring after a while."

"No doubt. You're a popular guy. All the wives and girlfriends keep trying to set you up."

"You planted someone in the cocktail circuit, didn't you?" I asked.

"I did. A psychiatrist. We've been keeping an eye on you, making sure you're up to working again."

"I have nine combat tours; you're worried about me falling apart over what happened?"

"I wasn't worried. Some people wanted to be sure."

"Are you going to make me guess who was spying on me?"

"Figure it out; let's see how good a detective you are."

"It was Linda Chaplin, Stan Chaplin's wife."

"That didn't take long. How did you figure?"

"Because of all the guys in the crowd, the only one I can't stand is Stan Chaplin."

"Why is that?"

"He's one of those guys who never seems to get tired of talking about himself; he finds a way to inject his history into every conversation. I always figured the reason his wife spent so much time talking with me was an excuse to get away from the self-centered boor. Now I'm guessing he was role-playing the one personality type I'm most tempted to choke out in a social situation."

"You nailed it. You've been profiled. Did a good job, too. Impulses are fully under control. You didn't toss the annoying bastard into the sea even while he was nonstop bragging to you about his many accomplishments in the Saudi Arabian oil business."

"I just ignored him; the rest of my drinking buddies are kind of fun."

"Not plants, they're genuine."

"You should've just sent Dr. Schneeberger over to examine me. She's my favorite head shrinker."

"She has a blind spot where you're concerned. We wanted someone objective to check under the hood."

"Linda played her role well. I might go to the party tonight and compliment her."

"She won't be there. Your vacation is over."

We were sitting in the living area on opposite couches. I swirled the small amount of wine remaining in my glass, waiting for Mike to continue. I took a sip emptying the glass and then refilled both of our drinks.

"Don't leave me in suspense. What's my next job?"

It took two hours for Mike to give me a general outline of the plan. When he was done, we went to dinner at Hakkasan, the Chinese restaurant at the hotel. We finished the night smoking Cohibas and drinking Cognac in the Cuban Bar. I loaned Mike my room in the Palace Hotel. The next morning, I found him sitting at the breakfast nook in the *Nomad's* galley.

I made myself a coffee and sat down across from him.

"How do you feel?" he asked.

"Good, how about you?"

"Not sure if it's the jet lag or the booze, but I woke up this morning exhausted."

"That's the jetlag."

"What's the big picture on this operation? What is it the big bosses are trying to accomplish?"

"They want you to destroy the ports and they want it to look like someone else did it."

"Yeah, I get that. But what's the point?"

"We're trying to discourage behavior."

"What kind of behavior?"

"Predatory lending behavior."

"What do you mean?"

"China loaned Montenegro money to build a highway

from its port on the Adriatic Sea to Serbia. Right now, the highway is less than half built and they have no chance of finishing it. Montenegro has taken on debt equivalent to 80% of its GDP to start the job and nobody is going to finance them to complete the job. Montenegro will never be able to repay. China effectively owns Montenegro.

"Kenya accepted a ton in loans from China to build the Standard Gauge Highway stretching from Mombasa to Nairobi. Kenya is now in default, China is foreclosing and is taking over Kenya's Mombasa seaport in exchange for loan forgiveness.

"Sri Lanka is so over-indebted to China that they were just forced to give a ninety-nine-year lease of the Hambantota seaport to a Chinese company owned by the Chinese Government.

"Pakistan embraced the China-Pakistan Economic Corridor, using debt provided by China. With debt to China at $19 billion and rising, Pakistan will never be able to pay it off. China wants an overland link to Pakistan's warm-water deep-sea port at Gwadar on the Arabian Sea. In exchange for loan restructuring, Pakistan granted another Chinese state-owned enterprise ownership of Gwadar's port."

"It's like Payday loans on a global scale."

"Exactly; it's how China is expanding its dominance and it has to stop."

"We force the Chinese to either give up the loan shark gains or we back them up with military force. That's the plan?"

"Yes, that's the plan. We believe that if the local people reject Chinese economic conquest of their national resources it will discourage what, up to this point, has been a very successful expansion tactic for the Chinese."

"Sounds good to me."

CHAPTER 20

DUBAI, UAE

I MET THE TEAM at the Marina in Dubai. I docked next to the Address Hotel in the late afternoon and met Migos, McDonald, and Savage in the lobby. I walked them the hundred yards from the back exit of the hotel to the Marina and out to my new yacht.

"*Wayward Nomad*, how did you come up with that one?" Migos said.

"That name was assigned by the Agency."

"I think they may have had me in mind when they picked it; are you sure this isn't my boat?"

"You're going to have to take my word for it. If you want a boat, sell the Emperor's gold and buy your own."

"I can't. I'm fully invested, I found a woman who's a genius at real estate."

"Tell me that's not true," I said, as we walked inside the salon.

"It is. I'm going to be the next Donald Trump."

"Let me guess; she's hot."

"Smoking. I would never invest with an ugly woman;

they're bitter and they only want to punish people because of it."

"That's a fool-proof investment strategy, Migos. You should've talked to someone who knows what they're doing before blowing your pirate stash on a bimbo with a real estate license."

"She's not a bimbo, she's famous; she even does her own infomercials," Migos said, as the three of them occupied the couches in the salon of the yacht."

"Enough on the real estate business. Tomorrow morning we're going to set sail for Kenya. Our task is to shut down the Mombasa Port and make it look like it was a terrorist group that did it."

"Rolling up in a ten-million-dollar yacht and wreaking havoc on the biggest port in Kenya is a good way to draw attention."

"We're not going to launch operations from the *Nomad*. We're just going to use it to get into the country with the equipment we need to do the job."

"The equipment is already on board?"

"It is."

"We'll stage off the yacht, but the plan is we conduct a series of infils to shut down the Port every time they get it running again."

"Why are we doing that?"

"Our new reason for existence is to become a hindrance to China's Belt and Road Initiative or Silk Road or whatever they call their imperialistic plan to conquer the world. We are going to level the playing field by targeting the gains the Chinese are making illegally."

"How was the Mombasa Port gained illegally?"

"The Mombasa Port was a debt trap; they sucked the Kenyans into over-borrowing with the intent of gaining a deep-water naval port in East Africa when the Kenyans defaulted, which they did. Our goal now is to make the acquisition costlier than the Chinese expected."

"How do we do that?"

"By doing what we do best, and that's to blow shit up."

"That I understand," replied Savage and Migos simultaneously.

"We're going to blow up the Mombasa Port?" asked McDonald.

"Nothing dramatic. We're not going to destroy the whole thing, just disrupt operations every now and again to make the operation a big money loser for the Chinese."

"That's it?"

"Yes, you have to understand, the Chinese have a whole bunch of dirty operations we're going to throw sand in the gears on. We hit the Mombasa Port a couple of times and before long, they'll have to station a thousand soldiers to guard it. We do that everywhere, and eventually, it becomes too costly for the Chi-Coms to maintain the empire."

"Is it just us conducting these operations?"

"I have no idea; I know better than to ask. You should all know that if you ever let on what we're doing to someone other than us, it would be a very serious problem for all of us."

"What else?" Migos asked.

"The Chinese sell billions in consumer products to an organized crime Triad that operates under government protection in China. The Triad then ships the items to Greece, where they bribe and intimidate the Greek government officials in order to register the product values at a tiny fraction of the real value. By doing that, they dodge hundreds of millions of Euros each year in tariffs. From Greece, they transport the goods within the EU and sell the products easily, because nobody who pays the full tariffs can compete against them on price. The Chinese Triad in Greece is going to be our next target."

"How many targets do you have?"

"Five to start with, but the list is very long."

"You have a lot of anger toward the Chinese at the moment; maybe you should see someone."

"I think my emotional state is the reason we drew this operation; the Agency wants me to channel my hostility in a constructive manner."

CHAPTER 21

BEIJING, CHINA

HUANG HAD BEEN sitting patiently in the waiting room of the Minister of State Security for two hours. He stood and signaled to the secretary that he was going to the men's room. Once inside, he lit a cigarette and stared at his reflection in the mirror. His suit hung off his body and the collar of his shirt was a full inch too large for his neck. His crew cut was peppered with grey. He exhaled a long plume of smoke at the mirror and watched as his face came into focus. His nose was flat; the bones had been crushed so severely it now looked like a lump of clay. The Americans had repaired his jaw and while it retained most of its former square shape, it now remained slightly ajar and hurt when he ate. He finished his cigarette and returned to reception to await his fate.

It was after five when the Minister finally called him in. Huang entered the office and stood in front of the Minister's desk. The Minister invited him to sit with a hand gesture.

Soundlessly, a servant entered the office and placed a cup of tea on the desk in front of Huang.

"How are you feeling?" the Minister inquired in a soft tone.

"I feel good. I'm ready to get back to work."

"I apologize for the lengthy interrogation on your return to China. I'm sure you understand its protocol."

"Yes, Minister, I understand completely."

"How did the Americans treat you?"

"They provided medical attention and fixed my wounds. I was shot, badly beaten, and unconscious when I was taken. They withheld pain killers and interrogated me with chemicals for days. I don't know what information I gave them, but I fear it was a lot."

"We recalled every asset you had in the US as soon as we suspected you were captured. We knew what to expect. The damage was minimized."

"I failed, Minister. I hope you will accept my apology."

"You didn't fail, Huang. You discovered the PLA was concealing the true cause of the tsunami from the President. You tracked down the people who created the tsunami and identified the government and agency they worked for. You discovered a Chinese Intelligence defector the PLA was hiding. You found and killed the traitor. You didn't accomplish everything I sent you to do, but you didn't fail. On the contrary, you brought great credit to the MSS."

"I serve at your will, Sir," Huang said while bowing his head.

"Yes, you do, and that service is not yet finished. I went through a lot of trouble to get you back. After you were taken, I had more than a dozen Americans arrested, including the daughter of a Silicon Valley billionaire on drug charges in Hong Kong. The Americans were more than happy to trade for your release."

"I'm ready, sir; what is my next assignment?"

"The Americans have begun to sabotage the Roads and Belts Initiatives. The deep-water port we acquired in Mombasa, Kenya, has been attacked twice in the last three months. The port is losing money and barely usable. In the first attack, all of the heavy cranes used to load ships were destroyed with explosives. In the second attack, all of the customs warehouses were burned to the ground. Many of our commercial goods shipments to the European Union through Greece have been disrupted. We are experiencing similar problems in Pakistan and Sri Lanka."

"What do you want me to do?"

"I created a Task Force to deal with the problem. Brigadier Cheng, the Commander of the Task Force, is not making sufficient progress. He lacks your analytical skills and natural skepticism. He doesn't believe there is a connection. Instead, he attributes the problems we are having to isolated local rebel groups hostile to a Chinese presence; I disagree. I have relieved Cheng of Command; you are now in charge of the Task Force. Study these attacks, find out who is behind them, and put a stop to them."

"Yes, sir."

"You're dismissed."

"Yes, sir."

"And Huang. The next time I see you make sure you're wearing attire suitable to your position. I don't expect a Brigadier General in The Ministry of State Security to look like a homeless peasant."

"Yes, sir," Huang replied, as he let his sudden promotion to brigadier sink in.

CHAPTER 22

SIARGAO, PHILIPPINES

I WAS SITTING AT the dark wooden bar watching an endless loop of surfing. Loose Keys Bar was packed and the crowd was festive despite it being only a little after eight on a Monday night in the middle of March. I was drinking a San Miguel listening to a Filipino band do a decent imitation of Hotel California. Loose Keys Moto Culture draws more than its share of hipsters from what is fast becoming the hottest surf spot on the planet.

I was surrounded by a mixture of local islanders, hard-core surfers, and college-aged backpackers. The music was good. The beer was cold. The atmosphere was what can best be described as South Pacific chill, and my mind was preoccupied with how I was going to kill a man in Athens. After a day on Cloud 9, the point break that put Siargao on the map, I found a message on my phone from David Forrest.

Clearwater, the joint venture between David and me, had been generating target lists for our ongoing operation against the Chinese. The latest man to make that list was Andre Onassis, a member of the Greek Parliament who'd just received a very large deposit in his bank account from the Government of China. Andre had the influence to erase all of the work my team had been doing over the past couple of months to restore law and order to the tariff systems in Greece for Chinese goods. Mr. Onassis was obviously of the opinion that he was beyond our reach. Trident had killed the Chinese Triad leadership operating in Athens in some of the most spectacular and news-catching ways. After the example had been set with the Triad, we merely had to whisper what would happen to the various government functionaries if they continued to break the law and give the Chinese an unfair market advantage.

Onassis had been reached by someone outside of the Triad and now, according to David, he was going to put an even greater fear into the hearts and minds of the pliable civil servants he needed to certify bogus Chinese paperwork. I signaled for another beer as I considered why Mr. Onassis would do such a thing. The drummer launched into the drum intro of "Two Princes" by the Spin Doctors which distracted me a bit as I began to mentally list the biggest hits that began with drum intros. Two of the guys I surfed with earlier in the afternoon came by and said "Hello." They were Australian and both were good enough to be here in the fall when the international surf competition is held.

Onassis wouldn't take the risk unless he was promised protection. Knowing the lethality and mendacity of the Triad, he had to know the threat he was signing up against was a serious one. Mr. Onassis either had a death wish, was being blackmailed, or had been promised protection by someone with serious power—or maybe it was a combination of factors. We would find out soon enough.

David was working up a target package. Before the week was over, we would know everything there was to know about Onassis. David's surveillance capability was so good that every electronic device Onassis carried would have been turned into a camera, microphone, and GPS locating device that would be broadcasting full time all there was to know about our next victim. Whoever was protecting him had better be good. I bought a bucket of beers for my surf buddies who were taking a table on the far side of the room. They waved for me to join them, but I signaled my thanks and stayed where I was. By ten, they were joined by two hipster girls and began to rotate onto the increasingly crowded dance floor. I got up off my stool and walked out into the humid night. The town of Grand Luna was dark, surrounded by ocean on one side and the jungle on the other three sides. I walked away from the sound of the surf and music and headed deeper into the town. A hundred yards in, I found a path that was lined with small trees. As I wove through the trees, I could hear the noise of a crowd. I walked into an opening and found the building. Kermit's Restaurant and Surf Resort, the sign said. I sat down at my usual table and when Beth, the waitress, came over, I asked for the Scaloppine al Marsala and sautéed vegetables. I told her to surprise me with the wine; Kermit's has a surprisingly good wine cellar for a surfing resort on a remote Philippine island. I like to arrive late because the restaurant doesn't accept reservations and the waiting line can sometimes exceed an hour. The food in Kermit's is outstanding—my chicken was perfect and the Chianti sublime. I paid the bill as they were closing at eleven and headed back toward the sound of the surf.

I considered calling it a night and returning to my room on the beach but decided on a nightcap at Rhum bar. I walked the four hundred yards west along the beach road away from the town. The road is pitch black with no traffic. I can hear the Reggae music and the crowd as I approach. It's an open bar filled with partiers. As I enter, Jessa, a pretty Filipina waitress, magically finds a stool from somewhere and makes a space for me at the bar. Without asking, Jessa places a frosty San Miguel Pale Ale on the counter in front of me. As I sit down, I decide the best way to deal with Mr. Onassis was to take him out the next time he was going to vote at Parliament. He couldn't take his Chinese protection with him into the Hellenic Parliament Building. It would make it easy to find him and it would send the message loud and clear that if you take bribes from the Chinese there was no place safe to hide. I spin my stool around and face the beach crowd on the dance floor. It's a crazy group of revelers; the band plays an eclectic mix of reggae, pop, and rock to a convulsing throng of vacationers, locals, and surfers every night until dawn.

After a few beers, I walk back toward the town. I'm staying at a beach hut at a place called the Isla Cabana in town. It's a basic room; I step over my surfboard on the way to the bed. I'm asleep as soon as I hit the bed. The next morning, the first thing I do is call David and task him with the information I need to get access to Onassis. I walked to the Deli Street Café and had breakfast. It's a cool bohemian-themed place that has an amazing breakfast and the best coffee in Siargao. After breakfast, I mount the surfboard on the side of my scooter and head out to Pacifica on the northern tip of the island in search of double overhead left-handed barrels. I didn't check the surf report because I know that as long as there isn't an inland wind, the conditions would be good.

I rode my scooter with surfboard mounted on the right side down a narrow dirt jungle road for forty-five minutes. I was wearing shorts, sandals, and sunglasses. When I reached the beach, I was the only person there. The break was out beyond the reef and it looked small from the distance, but I knew it wouldn't be.

I paddled my board for a thousand yards out to the break and then another two hundred yards through it. The waves were twelve feet high and it took a real effort to get past the surf. From Siargao, the Pacific Ocean extends without the interference of any major land masses all the way to California. The prevailing westerly winds create swells that travel for thousands of miles across the ocean, past the hidden depths of the Philippine Trench before breaking against the gently sloped sands of Siargao. Sitting on my board, beyond the break, I was all alone and I felt a million miles from the rest of the world.

I spied a set of rollers that I liked and oriented my board toward the beach. I let the first one pass and used the knowledge gained from watching it break to better position myself. When the second one came, I paddled hard and thrust myself toward the beach as I felt the power of the wave under me. I popped up onto the board in a crouch as it plunged down into the barrel. I carved a left turn and stayed inside the barrel of the tube facing away from the wave. The view of the beach was blocked by the waters cascading over me, creating a green prism to the outside world. Gradually, the tube closed around me, and I was engulfed by the warm frothy waters. I cut rapidly back to the ocean on my board and sailed into the sky as my board fell away from under my feet.

I repeated the same process for the next three hours. I was hungry and thirsty when I finally made my way back to the beach. I loaded up my board and headed back on my scooter. Less than a mile down the beach road on the way to Grand Luna, I stopped at the Bollox Bar for lunch. I sat outside on a plastic patio chair and ordered a cheeseburger, large bottle of water, and a beer. Under the shade of an umbrella on the beach, I downed the water in seconds and ordered a second one. Bollox Bar is a blue cinderblock building on the edge of a deserted beach that is the epitome of the island getaway. It's owned by a Brit who escaped western civilization decades earlier. It's off the beaten path on an island that is already the very definition of off the beaten path. After a day in the waves, Bollox Bar is the ideal place to eat lunch, drink beer, and even take a nap.

It was almost five by the time I got back to my room in Grand Luna. When I checked my phone, I had a bunch of missed calls. I called David first, then I returned the call from Mike.

"Don't you carry your phone anymore?"

"I was surfing; phones don't work well under water."

"My people have been talking to Dave Forrest. He's making strange information requests. What are you planning?"

"I haven't decided anything. You're going to have to trust me on this." If I told Mike I was going to kill a member of Parliament— of a NATO partner no less— he would have to get it approved all the way up to the President. There was absolutely no chance anyone in Washington, DC, would ever entertain the killing of a Greek politician, especially inside the Hellenic House of Parliament. Onassis was counting on that fact in the same way he was counting on the Greek law that prohibited members of Parliament from being charged with a crime. He was making a mistake.

The next flight out wasn't until the morning, and so I decided to go to Loose Keys for a beer and repeat my evening routine. I dropped by the front desk and gave the hotel a small stack of pesos to hold my room for another month. After the job was finished, I planned to return and stay until the rainy season and then I would move on to somewhere else.

CHAPTER 23

ATHENS, GREECE

I STEPPED OFF THE ferry in Athens and signaled a taxi. I found a restaurant outside the Parliament building and ordered breakfast. I stroked my fake beard and looked out the window at the park. I finished my coffee and headed out to the Parliament building. I crossed the street and threaded my way through the protestors. It was cold and they were few in number and bundled up in heavy jackets. I couldn't read the Greek protest signs, but I imagined they were about the country's economic situation, which was a mess. I found the visitors' entrance and joined the line.

The guard checked my passport and the second guard patted me down after I passed through the metal detector, even though it didn't signal. I followed the rest of the visitors up the stairs and found a seat high up in the balcony viewing area. My seat was three stories above the assembled Parliament. I watched for two hours as the governing body deliberated, unable to understand a single word of the debate. There are three hundred members of Parliament and it looked like all of them were present and had something to say about everything. It took me twenty minutes before I spotted Andre Onassis seated in a front bench. I couldn't figure out how the seating was arranged, whether it was by party or by position. I read that Onassis was a leader in the Communist party, which seemed about right for someone so greedy and corrupt.

When the Parliament adjourned, I made my way downstairs to the second floor and went in search of Onassis's office. David had done a good job providing me with the details of the building. I walked slowly to the end of the corridor where his office was located. I hunched my shoulders and kept my movements consistent with the grey wig, beard, and glasses I was wearing.

When I entered the office, I was greeted by a heavy-set receptionist. Two other men in suits were sitting in the waiting area.

"I have an appointment with Mr. Onassis; is he in?" I asked.

"May I have your name, sir?" the woman replied in excellent English.

"Stanley Harrison."

The woman looked at the calendar on her computer and turned back to me.

"I'm sorry, Mr. Harrison, but you are not on the schedule. Please leave your contact information and I will ask if Mr. Onassis wants me to schedule an appointment."

"Miss, it is imperative that I see him. Could you please let him know that I am here and that I have news from Yan Shunkai? He is sure to want to see me, as Yan is the leader of a Chinese Triad and he recently paid Mr. Onassis three million euros to smuggle Chinese goods into the EU."

I made sure to speak loud enough for the two gentlemen in the waiting area to hear me.

The receptionist looked flustered. She picked up the phone and spoke in Greek to someone. I didn't wait for an answer. I continued through the wooden double doors into the inner office where I found another secretary and several offices. From the placard on the center one, it was easy to find where Onassis worked.

"I'm going in to see Mr. Onassis." The secretary didn't attempt to stop me. I shuffled to the door with my stooped question mark-shaped back and walked through the open door. Inside, I found Onassis and another man about the same age as the MP. Onassis said something to me, but I wasn't paying attention. I was scanning the top of his desk.

"Are you involved in the bribes Onassis is taking from the Chinese Government?" I asked the man standing next to Onassis.

"What are you talking about? Get out of here. Who do you think you are?" the man demanded. While the man was protesting my presence, I picked up a letter opener from Onassis's desk and drove the blade upward under his chin and into the brain of Mr. Onassis. Before the other man could even process what was happening, I struck him hard with a downward blow with my right hand. I pulled a pair of leather driving gloves from my heavy winter overcoat and put them on. Then I removed a handkerchief and wiped down the handle of the paper opener that was sticking out of Onassis' throat.

I wiped and locked the office door before I exited. The secretary eyeballed me as I shuffled past her but did not say anything. I walked past the receptionist and received the same hostile body language. Once inside the corridor, I took the first set of stairs down to the first floor. I maintained my posture and foot speed even though, with each passing second, I was worried the man I hit in the office would regain consciousness and sound the alarm or the secretary would unlock the door.

I made it past security and through the visitor entrance door into the cold Athens afternoon. I picked up my gait as I moved off the Parliament grounds. Behind the building is a huge park. The front of the Parliament building is a football-field-sized open concrete area that serves as the visitors' entrance and also houses a couple of memorials. I reached the main avenue and crossed. Once across the street, I turned left and then, after fifty yards, turned right at a side street. I found the public restroom and, after checking for cameras, I entered the men's lavatory. I was alone in the small men's room. I removed my wig, beard, and glasses and threw them into the trash dispenser. I took off my heavy, long black overcoat and hung it in the toilet stall. I left the men's room looking much younger and clean shaven, wearing a blue patterned fleece jacket and a baseball cap.

I continued along the same road, walking toward the Acropolis. I found a taxi and told him to take me to the Athens Port. I paid the cabbie in cash and walked down the pier to my charter. The boat ride to Kythnos took two hours. I spent the time inside the warm cabin reading magazines. When we finally docked, I was thrilled to see not a single police officer. I found a taxi and had them take me to the marina on the other side of the island where I had the *Nomad* tied up.

The boat ride to Paphos, Cyprus, was a twelve-hour trip, but I was only at sea for less than an hour when I got a call from Mike on my satphone.

"Where are you?"

"I'm about an hour west of Rhodes, heading home."

"Jesus, I cannot believe you did that."

"What are you hearing out of Athens?"

"MP Onassis was murdered in his office. The man who killed him was a tall, English-speaking elderly man with a beard. Witnesses heard him accuse the MP of accepting bribes from the Chinese Government to cover up a Chinese smuggling operation. Another MP was in Onassis's office during the attack. He was knocked unconscious and is in the hospital receiving treatment for a concussion. A massive manhunt is underway."

"Rumor has it, the vigilante got away."

"Rumor has it."

"I'll bet the next MP the Chinese make an offer to passes on the deal."

"The one place the Chinese can't provide security is inside the Parliament building. I'm guessing they've identified that weakness by now."

"Ya think?"

"What are your plans?"

"Back to surfing in Siargao, then to wherever Dave sends me and the boys. I'm guessing Karachi; we've slowed down things enough in Kenya and Greece for a while."

"You didn't take any of the boys?"

"No, I didn't want them involved. Easier this way if something went wrong."

"Did anything go wrong?"

"No, I don't think so. Although I don't plan on coming back to Greece anytime soon."

"Good idea. I'll let you know if your name comes up anywhere."

"What are you going to tell your higher-ups?"

"Nothing."

"Nothing? They'll figure it out if they haven't already, but it's best to leave it alone."

"Yup, never happened."

"Never happened."

The rest of the trip to Cyprus went without a hitch. I used a different marina because everyone at the Paphos Marina knew me on sight. After clearing customs, I tied up at a slip in the Limassol Marina, which is thirty miles east of Paphos. Unlike the Paphos Marina that has its fair share of fishing and work vessels, the Paphos Marina is filled with yachts and even a few super yachts. It was evening by the time I finished fueling and completed the after-operation maintenance. I slept with a pistol under my pillow just in case my cover wasn't as good as I thought it was.

I rented a car at the nearby Yacht Club and drove to the Trident office at Paphos Airport. It was a beautiful late winter morning; the sun was shining, and it was seventy degrees by mid-morning when I pulled up next to the hangar. I found the guys loading the C-130J with pallets of ammunition crates when I walked in. The ramp on the aircraft was down and pallets were being loaded into it with a remote control Palfinger forklift. I watched for a couple of minutes and then walked over to the guys who were building air pallets.

"Why are you rebuilding the pallets?" I asked.

"They came with like items, but they want us to deliver mixed packs."

"I guess that makes sense. Where is this load heading?"

"Benghazi."

I went around and talked with the crew. Eventually, I watched the ramp come up and our tug pulled the aircraft outside the hangar. The four turboprops on the big black Hercules came to life, and the plane rolled down the tarmac toward the runway. I caught up with Migos and McDonald in the break area located off to the side of the massive hangar interior.

"What have you been up to, boss?"

"Surfing Cloud-9 in Siargao. What about you?"

"Working and waiting on you to give us our next assignment."

"Wait's over. The next mission is in Gwadar, Pakistan, about ten miles from the Iranian border."

"What are we going to do to Gwadar?" McDonald asked.

"Same thing we did in Kenya; we're going to make the port unusable."

"That shouldn't be too tough."

"It will be harder. Gwadar is the end of the overland route from China to the Arabian Sea. The Chinese are building an oil pipeline so that a conflict in the South China Sea where 100% of their oil supplies currently travel can have an alternate route in case of crisis."

"What does that mean to us?"

"It means that, unlike the last port that was guarded by a handful of drug-using untrained Africans, Gwadar is protected by over a thousand Chinese private security guards."

"I can see where that might be a problem," Migos said.

"We'll figure it out. I've asked David to fly in today and do the intel for us. We'll spend the next few days hammering out a plan and then prepping."

"Sounds good," McDonald chirped in.

CHAPTER 24

BEIJING, CHINA

HUANG WAVED TO the receptionist on the way into the Minister of State Security's office. He was a frequent visitor and she knew to wave him through without delay. He was often running up the four flights of stairs to visit the Minister two or three times a day. Despite his position in the Chinese hierarchy, the Minister was convinced all of his electronic communications were being monitored by Chinese Intelligence, which is why he relied on face to face meetings as much as possible.

"Did you find anything?" the Minister asked, as Huang was sitting down on the couch in the office seating area.

"I believe the man who killed Onassis was Pat Walsh." Huang subconsciously rubbed his crooked jawline at the mention of Walsh.

"It was a CIA hit, then?"

"Yes, definitely."

"Can you prove it was Pat Walsh?"

"Not completely. The only evidence on the scene is

some camera footage taken inside the Parliament building and some outside. He was disguised in both."

"Then what makes you think it was Pat Walsh?"

"I took a lot of surveillance footage on Walsh in the Bahamas."

"Where are you going with this?"

"The man who killed Onassis had glasses and a thick beard, making facial recognition impossible. I ran the footage from Greece and the footage from the Bahamas through a gait analysis program. The footage taken inside the Parliament building had a 20% matching value. The footage taken outside the building had a 92% match; he must have been disguising his walk when he was inside, but once outside, he had to hurry and discarded the deception."

"If we tested every person in the world, how many would have a 92% or higher match probability?" asked the Minister.

"Millions, possibly as many as a hundred million, is my guess."

"Gait analysis is not very conclusive then, is it?"

"Combined with everything else we know about Walsh, it's a much stronger case that it was him."

"There was nothing else, fingerprints, DNA, anything at all?"

"No, Minister."

"Ever since Eleuthera, you've had a fixation on Walsh. Keep an open mind on this; follow facts and evidence. Don't fall into the trap of trying to fit the evidence to a premature conclusion."

"Yes, Minister. I hope it is acceptable that I have

returned surveillance to his home in Eleuthera and his marina and hangar in Paphos, Cyprus."

"That's fine. But remember, the problem is the entire CIA and possibly the US military; it's much bigger than Pat Walsh."

"My net is large, sir."

"These attacks against our assets in Africa, Asia, and Europe are becoming very expensive, both politically and economically. We need to put a stop to them."

"How do we do that? We can't intercept every attack."

"We need to catch the Americans in the act of sabotaging one of their allies or a friendly nation's transportation assets and then we need to expose what they are doing to the world. We will humiliate them and create an international relations scandal; that will force them to stop."

"We could always counter-attack."

"We've been doing that. Your job is defense. Leave the offense to others."

"I've been working on a defensive strategy."

"What do you have?"

"I don't think they'll hit Mombasa, Djibouti, or Athens again for a while. They've had a sufficient amount of success on those targets and it wouldn't make sense to attack them again in the near future. I'm concentrating my agents on the transit point in Malaysia, Pakistan, Laos, and Cambodia. I intend to pick them up on their infiltration and then catch them in the act of sabotage. I'm confident we will be successful."

"We need to succeed. The Americans are getting very aggressive. They've moved three carrier strike groups into the South China Sea and they're backing the territorial rights to the Spratlys by Vietnam and Philippines. We're not even able to access the reefs to begin reconstruction."

"I won't disappoint you, Minister."

"I know you won't, Huang."

Huang left the Minister's office more committed than ever.

CHAPTER 25

INDIAN OCEAN

OUR C130 LIFTED off at midnight on a flight that was cleared from Dhafra Air Force Base in UAE to Mumbai, India. We'd spent the previous night inside the Trident hangar, well within the protection of the perimeter fence of the UAE's largest Air Force Base. For years we'd been supplying the Kurdish Peshmerga and other American allies fighting ISIS from our Dhafra facility that had been generously donated for that purpose by the UAE Government, who were equally invested in eradicating ISIS. We don't use the Dhafra hangar as much as we used to, but it's still a comfortable place to stage out of when necessary.

The Hercules was flying on a southeast heading. We crossed over from UAE to Oman and then over the Gulf of Oman. Our time to target was just under two hours. Gwadar Port is located almost directly across the Gulf of Oman from Muscat. From my seat, I watched Sachse, the flight loadmaster, stick all of his fingers up into the air to signal the ten-minute warning. The interior lights turned to red and the back ramp of the C130 started to open. We were flying five thousand feet above the Gulf which meant the cabin was pressurized and that there would be no need for oxygen masks.

McDonald, Savage, and I connected our parachute static lines to a metal cable that ran the length of the cargo compartment. The four of us were up almost as far as the cockpit because most of the cargo area was filled with a black twenty-four-foot midget submarine that was propped up on a Marine Craft Aerial Delivery (MCAD) System. The four-ton swimmer delivery vehicle (SDV) was shaped like a pregnant torpedo and was resting on the MCAD, which is little more than an aluminum sled used to brace the six-man underwater boat and keep it upright while it's on a solid surface. The floor of the C-130 cargo bay has two rows of parallel steel rollers that'll allow the flat aluminum base of the MCAD to roll smoothly out the cargo door with minimum resistance.

From my position as the lead jumper, I watched Sachse release the tie-downs on both sides of the MCAD. The wiry Kentuckian crawled on top of the SDV and played with the chutes rigged on top of the sub. Sachse pulled out a small bundle of green silk from a sealed compartment and slid down to the cargo floor. The Hercules was traveling at a hundred and thirty-five knots and the noise of the engines and the rush of the air made it difficult to hear the thirty-second warning when it came over my headset.

With his arm extended toward the open cargo door, Sachse let the tiny parachute canopy fly into the rushing air. The extractor parachute flew out the rear cargo door and snapped open when the cord that was anchored to the SDV played out to its full length, thirty feet behind the aircraft.

The SDV sprang into motion, quickly picking up speed as it slid over the rollers and launched into the night sky. I chased after the SDV until I, too, was outside of the aircraft and falling. When I felt the sharp jerk of my parachute opening, I reached up above my shoulders and grabbed the steering toggles. I turned left when I spotted the three billowing chutes of the SDV. Beneath the cargo parachutes, I could see the marking lights on the SDV and when I looked closer to the surface, I could just barely make out the smaller parachute holding the freshly separated MCAD.

The moon was bright, and it was easy to follow the SDV down to the sea. I knew McDonald and Savage were above and slightly behind me. I heard the belly-flop sound of the sub hitting the water. I hoped the water-activated floats kicked into action, otherwise getting the sub into operation was going to be a lot harder.

I unclipped most of my rigging before reaching the water. The moment my fleet splashed into the warm Gulf, I released my leg straps and then my chest strap. I was free of my parachute harness while still plunging down into the depths. As soon as my descent stopped, I crawled upward toward the light of the moon making sure to break the surface a distance from my parachute. I took a big breath of air and then looked around for the SDV. The water was rough, and it took me a moment to find the green marker light. I had to find a time when I was riding up on a swell and had some visibility. It was only seventy-five yards to the SDV and because I was wearing just a wetsuit and a plastic bump helmet, I covered the distance quickly. When I reached the SDV, I climbed on top and began to remove the parachute rigging. I could see the marking lights of McDonald and Savage coming my way and before long all three of us were prepping the SDV for operation. While on top of the SDV, I opened the forward hatch and allowed McDonald to slide into the partially-submerged control compartment. He put on the full-face diving mask that was connected to the onboard air system. The mask was also connected to the SDV internal and radio communications system. McDonald began to power up the systems including the obstacle avoidance radar, GPS, inertial navigation system, and the four cameras that surrounded the sub. After a few minutes, he told us over our comm sets to begin releasing the supplemental buoyancy packs. Savage and I donned the rest of our scuba gear and began pulling the quick releases on each side of the sub to set the buoyancy packs loose.

When we were done, barely a foot of the SDV was riding above the water. Every ten or fifteen seconds the SDV would drop into a trough and we'd have to hold on tight as an ocean swell would sweep over the top of the midget sub.

"Ready to load," I said over my radio to McDonald, while trying to time the movement of the ocean.

The passengers' compartments in the aft of the SDV slid open and Savage and I jumped in on each side. The SDV was filled with water. Through my mask, I could see McDonald at the front of the SDV with his hand on the joystick controller. There were no windows on the SDV, and the only lights came from the bright console in front of McDonald and the ring of control lights around it for the various systems. As soon as I got in, I grabbed the full-face SDV mask mounted on my right side. I put it on, cleared the mask of water, and looked over to check on Savage to my left.

"Is everybody good to go?" I asked.

"I'm up," Savage said.

"Ready," McDonald replied.

"Let's hope the rest of this op goes as well," I said.

"Don't jinx it," the impassive Savage replied.

"Ok, McDonald, it's all you," I said, as the door next to me slid shut.

The Huntington-Ingalls Proteus SDV has a maximum speed of ten knots and a cruising speed of eight knots. The trip into Pakistani waters and onto Gwadar Port was going to take us ninety minutes. The passenger compartment in the SDV is nothing more than a webbed seat in the back of a dark coffin. Between the passenger compartment and the driver's compartment was an open cargo area that held our gear for the operation, but still allowed us to see McDonald. In a matter of minutes, we were moving at cruising speed and diving to our planned traveling depth of fifty feet.

The Proteus can be armed with several different weapons systems including mines, the Common Rapid Attack Weapon (CRAW), which is used to defeat a torpedo attack, and the Common Very Light Weight Torpedo (CVLWT), which can be used against submarines and surface ships. Unfortunately, we got this Proteus on loan from the CIA and it didn't come with any ammunition. The Proteus we were using is a prototype built for a competition that was held to replace the US Navy SEALS Mach VIII in 2015. A different vehicle made by Teledyne Brown won the competition, which then allowed the CIA to take the Proteus prototype off of the manufacturer's hands.

"We're five minutes out," McDonald said over the radio system.

I removed my mask and replaced it with the regulator and mask from my scuba set-up. The Nitrox gas mix was the same. I slid on a climbing harness and then buckled on my BCD with the connected air cylinder and put on my fins. I hooked my backpack and rifle to my climbing harness and slid out a SUEX dive scooter from the cargo compartment.

The passenger doors opened and Savage and I each exited from opposite sides. I checked the NAV board on the scooter and headed due east. We slowly ascended as we advanced until we reached a depth of five feet. Savage followed directly behind me until I bumped up against a concrete pillar of a pier and then he joined me in holding onto it. Savage and I removed our weapons and slowly surfaced. We were brushing against a pillar that rose thirty feet to the pier above. Savage and I each tied our scuba equipment onto a rope we wrapped around the pillar and then we marked it with an InfraRed Chemlite.

Savage pulled a REBS mini launcher out of his backpack. I removed the ATLAS ascender from mine. Savage fought the current and got into a position to fire a grapnel hook onto the cement pier floor above. I heard a pneumatic shot and then Savage returned to me with the line and I threaded it into the ascender. With my backpack and rifle slung over my back, I connected the ascender to the climbing harness around my waist and hit the up switch. I slowly rose to the pier from the water. Once on top, I lowered the ascender back down for Savage to use. I pulled my ballistic helmet and night vision goggles from my pack back. In less than two minutes, Savage was beside me.

We were both out on the open on the flat empty pier. Our targets were the six giant cranes located along the empty cargo-handling area. The pier was enormous. There was a smaller cargo vessel tied up closer to the shore and the crane that was tending it was much smaller than the two-hundred-foot behemoths we had our sights on. Big cranes are necessary to load and unload large container vessels; without them, cargo can't move, and the port shuts down. Savage took off at a trot toward the shore. I did a quick scan for guards and then ran in the opposite direction toward the crane located at the very end of the pier.

I placed cutting charges on two of the four main support beams on the crane. I connected the two charges with det cord and then pulled the fuze igniter. The time fuze was connected to only one of the charges, but the det cord would make sure they would both explode together. I dashed to the next crane. I was setting the charges on the second crane when I heard gunfire from Savage's direction.

"What's your situation?" I asked Savage.

"Vehicle patrol spotted me on my way to the center crane. I have them pinned down, but I can see mounted reinforcements heading my way."

"I'll rig the demo on the middle crane. Can you hold them for a little while?"

"Yes."

The fight was intensifying—the gunfire sounding like firecrackers going off. I ran to the middle crane and put the charges in place. I cut the time fuze so it would last only a few minutes and then I screwed the igniter on and pulled it.

"I'll cover—you run for the water," I said over the radio net.

From the base of the crane, I started firing at the vehicles and where I could see the muzzle flashes that were firing at

Savage. I watched a blur make the fifty-yard sprint to the edge of the pier and disappear into the water. The fire was then all directed at me, but I was at least one hundred yards farther back than Savage was and the fire was too far out of range to be accurate. I saw a line of at least ten personnel advancing toward me while others provided a base of fire. Now that they were maneuvering, it was definitely time to go. I slapped another thirty-round magazine into my HK 416, pointed the IR laser beam at the advancing line, and emptied it in five trigger bursts. Then I replaced the mag and repeated the process as incoming rounds pinged all around me.

The guards were getting way too close for comfort. I sprang up from the prone position at the base of the crane and ran toward the water with everything I had. I saw green tracers flying in front of me. I pivoted as I reached the edge of the pier and fired a parting burst as I felt myself fall. I put my arms out to prevent myself from knifing too deep into the water and kicked to the surface as hard as I could. With my night vision goggles still on, I spotted the IR Chemlite only a few yards away. I held onto my rifle and side stroked it to the concrete pillar where I found Savage already wearing his SCUBA gear and his weapon at the ready pointed straight up. I dropped my backpack and slid into my gear. I clipped my backpack and rifle to my waist harness and retrieved my dive scooter from the securing line.

"Are you ready to go?" I asked Savage.

"On you."

Just then, the sound of a big explosion filled the night air. The explosion was followed by the metallic screech of the crane falling. I was hoping it was going to fall in the direction of the guards, but I wasn't completely sure it wasn't falling toward us. Out of curiosity, I waited until I heard the loud crash of it hitting the ground before diving.

I descended straight down into the water for twenty feet, using the pillar as my guide. Once I caught up with Savage, I aimed the scooter to the open water and took off at two knots. The sonar receiver on my scooter console registered the sonar pinger from the SDV and provided all the navigational guidance I needed to find McDonald. It took Savage and me only ten minutes to locate the sub. The visibility was really bad, and I didn't know I had found the black SDV until my scooter hit it. The passenger doors immediately opened and we both quickly felt our way inside. McDonald slid the doors closed as soon as we were onboard, and we went immediately to full throttle.

It took me a few minutes to untangle myself from my hastily-donned equipment in the darkness. Eventually, I rid myself of the regulator and scuba mask and connected myself again to the onboard air and communications system.

"Is anybody in pursuit?" I asked.

"Not yet, but I'm sure patrol craft will be converging on this area soon."

"Are you good, Savage?" I asked.

"Yeah, I'm fine. I hope they don't find the other charges."

I looked at the time on my dive computer. "The next one is going off in less than fifteen minutes. Looking for those charges would be a fool's errand."

"Agreed."

"Could you tell if those guards were Chinese or Pakis?" I asked.

"Chinese. I heard them yelling to each other."

"Somebody is going to have to tell dear leader they just lost another deep-water port until they can get some new cranes."

"Yeah, sucks to be them."

The black SDV cut silently through the Gulf of Oman. The only sound was the electrically-powered propeller behind me and the sound of my breathing.

"We're crossing into international waters," McDonald reported after a little over an hour.

"How are the batteries holding up?" I asked.

"We have more battery power than we have air," he replied.

"How much air do we have left?" I asked, with some concern in my voice.

"Another three hours at least."

"Don't scare me like that," I said.

I felt the SDV slow. McDonald slowly ascended the SDV. He hit a switch and raised the mast on top of the sub. The fifteen-foot periscope mast had a camera that gave McDonald a view of the surface.

"What's up?" I asked.

"I'm at the rendezvous point. I just wanted to confirm that it's the *Nomad*."

"Is it?"

"Yeah, I can see Migos on the stern. I'm going to need you guys to swim out and connect the winch hook."

Savage and I redonned our scuba gear. I could hear McDonald using the thrusters to position the SDV directly behind the *Nomad*. McDonald brought the SDV to the surface. Savage and I swam out and finned it to the *Nomad* that was positioned only twenty yards away.

Migos was standing on the back ramp holding a big hook. Savage came up to the ramp and Migos handed him the hook. I swam with Savage and helped him pull the heavy cable and hook to the SDV. He connected the hook to the forward lift point on the SDV and then we both swam back to the yacht.

We helped Migos position the heavy steel roller ramp into the water. Heavy floats kept the ramp from crushing the ramp of the yacht and provided a guide to get the SDV up and over the garage door and onto the main deck. All of the furniture had been removed from the stern to allow room for the sub. The twenty-four-foot-long SDV wasn't going to fit entirely on the deck; about six feet was going to extend over the tail once the winch hoisted it up.

Migos worked the winch and brought the SDV close to the yacht. Savage and I jumped back into the water and muscled the SDV into position on the loading ramp.

"Bring it up!" I yelled to Migos.

Slowly, the SDV was pulled from the water. The winch bolted to the stern deck made easy work of pulling the four-ton submarine from the water. Once we had it on the deck, McDonald got out of the forward compartment. The sub was still draining water when we began to brace it into position. Once it was braced, we threw a tarp over it and tied it down.

"I hope we don't run into rough seas," I said.

"It'll hold. It's time to head back to Cyprus," McDonald replied.

The three of us sat up on the flybridge grilling steaks and drinking Sam Adams beers as we headed south at cruising speed. The added four tons of the sub didn't alter the ride of the ninety-ton yacht very much. McDonald was behind the wheel at the helm station on the starboard side of the deck. Migos, Savage, and I were sitting around the table on the L-shaped couch on the opposite side of the deck. It was a warm, beautiful night, and this was about the best way I could think of to end a mission.

"Where are you heading when we get back? Are you going back to the edge of the world surfing?" Migos asked.

"Never underestimate the therapeutic benefits of surfing and drinking," I replied.

"So that's a yes, then."

"No, I have to go to Geneva, Switzerland."

"What's in Geneva?"

"I'm settling Cheryl's estate. I have to empty her stuff out of the vault and get it to the broker who is selling it for me."

"Where's the money going?" Savage asked.

"She left it to me. I'm going to take her share of the treasure and half of mine and gift it to Father Tellez's Foundation. He's going to give it to the Church in the Philippines. The money will go to helping poor kids."

"That's nice."

"Yeah, we're even going to have a statue placed in memory of Cheryl on the grounds of the Cathedral in Puerto Princesa, Palawan."

"Was Cheryl Catholic?" Migos asked.

"No, she was Buddhist. But for a gift of almost two hundred million dollars, the Palawan Archdiocese is flexible about these things. You should see the statue; it's an all-white eight-foot-tall porcelain Buddha sitting on an elephant."

"Seriously?"

"Yeah, it's a real work of art from the Qing Dynasty. The broker got it from Christie's Auction; it's called *A Dehua Seated Figure of Samantabhadra.*"

"What's a Samantabhadra?"

"Buddha has a trinity of some sort, and one of the forms is Samantabhadra. He's the Buddha of action. Which seemed most appropriate for Cheryl. It's a nice statue, and on the base will be her picture and a plaque memorializing her."

"That's a great idea."

"Yeah, I think so."

Over the next four days, we took shifts as we traveled from the Gulf of Oman to the Gulf of Aden through the Red Sea and the Suez Canal and into the Mediterranean.

CHAPTER 26

GWADAR, PAKISTAN

THE RANGE ROVER stopped in front of the wreckage of the crane closest to the pier entrance. Huang and the Commander of the Chinese private security firm left the driver and got out of the back seat and walked the rest of the way to the end of the pier. They stopped occasionally to study the damage. Huang didn't say anything to the other man until they were on the far end of the pier overlooking the sea.

"How did the men enter?"

"They leaped off the pier into the water when my men confronted them. We believe that's also how they came in."

"Don't you have diver protections systems?"

"When the Naval ships are docked, they always run a sonar to defend against divers. We don't have any sonar systems when the Navy isn't present."

"Where did they swim to when they jumped off the pier?"

"I don't know. We had patrol craft sweeping the area

with sonars within fifteen minutes of them entering the water. We didn't detect any divers."

"How do you think they got away? Did they board a boat nearby and escape?"

"There were no boats within 5 kilometers. We think they used a submarine."

"A submarine?"

"It's the only way they could've gotten out of the search area before the patrol boats arrived."

"How many men were there?"

"We only saw two, but there may have been more."

"How many men did you have that encountered them?"

"Four vehicle patrols of three men each."

"How many of your men were killed?"

"None."

"How many were wounded?"

"Two, one seriously."

"It doesn't sound as though your men put up much of a fight."

"My men fought bravely, Sir. It was night and my men were ambushed facing an unknown force."

"You're right; it's unfair to question your men. It's you who've failed. The most logical place to infiltrate a port is from the sea and despite being placed on high alert, you didn't have a single defense directed at the sea. I will make sure to point out your incompetence in my report."

"Sir, I had patrol boats in the water."

"You should've had an anti-diver sonar, you fool."

Huang was furious. He walked back to the sedan alone and left the dejected guard commander to brood. He used the travel time to the airport as an opportunity to analyze the situation. The use of demolitions and diving automatically caused him to draw a connection to Pat Walsh and his CIA paramilitary force. He scribbled in his notepad orders that he would issue regarding the start of a manhunt for Pat Walsh. If Pat Walsh used a submarine for the operation, that would be a major escalation in the hostilities, because it would mean he had help from the US Navy. Up until now, there was no proof of any US involvement in the attacks on the ports. The destruction of the pier reminded him of the destruction Walsh had delivered to his own face. The Minister wanted him on defense, but it was time to strike back. He would keep his plans secret and attack alone so the Minister wouldn't find out and stop him. Huang decided he would finish what he started in Eleuthera, only this time, he wouldn't risk trying to capture Walsh. He would just kill him.

CHAPTER 27

SWITZERLAND

IT WAS LATE in the afternoon when we docked the *Nomad* at Limassol Marina. The marina has a big crane that's used to move yachts into and out of the water. We used the crane to lift the SDV off the back deck of the Nomad and onto a rented flatbed. McDonald and Savage accompanied the SDV back to our hangar while Migos and I refueled and tied up the *Nomad*.

When we were finished hooking up the power and water, Migos and I inspected the damage done by the four-ton SDV on the teak decking.

"Damage isn't too bad," Migos said, pointing to some deep scratches along the edge.

"It's repairable. I thought it was going to be a lot worse."

"Where to now?"

"I have a charter booked for tomorrow to Switzerland. I'm free tonight. Do you want to try out one of these Limassol restaurants?

"Which one?"

"There's one I've been wanting to try. Columbia Steakhouse. It's supposed to be the best one in Cyprus."

I made reservations and Migos and I dressed for dinner. Columbia Plaza is only a quarter mile from the Limassol Marina, and we decided to walk. The waterfront is a tourist area and it's a nice place to walk when the weather is cooperative. We arrived early for our reservation and decided to have a drink in the attached cigar bar before being seated.

"I like this place," Migos said.

"It's owned by a Greek, but it's an American-style steakhouse with a sushi menu."

"Talk about a culture clash."

"This is a food destination for the chic world travelers. Unlike the working stiffs in Paphos, Limassol is home to lots of the beautiful people."

"You liked Paphos better?"

"My marina neighbors were fishermen and recreational boaters instead of the world- traveling yacht owners, which I liked. But they didn't have any internationally renowned restaurants either."

When we were seated, Migos and I both went with the chateaubriand; it was fantastic, as were the onion rings and the wine. After dinner, Migos drove back to his apartment in Paphos and I stayed on the boat. It was a cool night and I put on a light jacket and sat up on the flydeck and drank a couple of beers while watching the Bruins play the Capitals on my iPad. I love the end of the hockey season; first, because the players really seem to up their intensity level in the hunt for the playoffs, and second, because it means baseball season is right around the corner.

The next morning, I drove to Limassol. I parked my

truck next to the Trident warehouse and boarded a chartered G-5 that was parked nearby. The weather in the Geneva area was cold and windy. Snow was piled high around the runway in the isolated mountain vault. I was met by the ever-efficient Mr. Hofstadter, and together we drove to the Vault in his car. Once inside, I segregated twenty-eight of the thirty-six boxes and lined them up for shipping. Mr. Hofstadter's staff inventoried the boxes, fixed metal seals on the metal boxes, and carried them away. I was given a receipt for the boxes and their contents. As an extra service, the Vault would transship the boxes to a Rothschild Bank in Zurich and transfer them over to the custody of my coin broker.

The flight to Zurich Airport took only forty-five minutes. At the private aircraft terminal, I passed through passport control and customs without a hitch. I only had a small suitcase to clear and the customs agent didn't even inspect it. The passive security made me regret not bringing a pistol. I took a taxi to the Park Hyatt in downtown Zurich. It's a business hotel located in the Old Town near the lake on Beethoven Strasse. Check-in was speedy and because my next meeting wasn't for a couple of hours, I decided to go to the gym.

When I was finished with the free weights, I decided to go for a short run on the treadmill. The treadmills are all in a row, oriented toward the windows overlooking the lake. Because of the lighting, I could see my reflection clearly in the window. About 3 kilometers into my run, I noticed an Asian man behind me on one of the stationary bikes. He was wearing iPhone earbuds and he didn't look like he was paying any attention to me, but his face looked familiar. I couldn't remember where, but I had a sneaky suspicion I had seen the man somewhere before. I strained to remember if it was at the airport terminal or in the lobby check-in. I finished my five-kilometer jog and headed back to my room to shower and change for my next meeting.

I was wearing jeans and winter clothing including a black ski jacket, watch cap, and gloves when I exited the lobby. I chose the Park Hyatt because it's only two hundred yards from the coin dealer—or the antiquity broker, as he liked to be called. Paranoid from my experience in the gym, I was concerned that I might have a tail. I began my walk heading in the opposite direction of my destination. I turned left out of the hotel and walked up Beethoven Strasse. The street is one way, and I was walking against the traffic. I crossed an intersection and continued on past the Chinese Construction Bank. I used the windows in the neighboring Saxo bank to see if anyone was following me. There were very few pedestrians in the area; one of them was an Asian in a grey coat. There can't be that many Asians in Zurich; my paranoia kicked into full gear. What are the chances? I continued on my way for another hundred yards until I came to a parking garage. I ducked into the parking garage and stepped into the elevator. I got out on the third floor. Once outside the elevator, I positioned myself with my back against the wall between the stair exit and the elevator door and I waited.

I kept checking my watch. I decided I'd wait fifteen minutes before giving up and finding a different exit from the parking garage than the one I used to come in. One guy couldn't watch all of the exits and the garage appeared to open onto two different streets. As it turned out, I didn't have to wait that long. I heard footsteps coming up the stairs. The entry to the stairwell didn't have a door. I could hear a single set of leather shoes approaching on the cement stairs. I watched as a solidly-built Asian man stepped out from the staircase. He glanced to the right and was swiveling his head back towards me when I hit him with a solid left hook to the jaw. He dropped and then I pounced on him and pummeled the dazed man with a set of two lefts and a right until he was no longer moving.

I ran down the stairs and left the parking garage on a street parallel to Beethoven Strasse. I was doubling back in the direction of the Park Hyatt. I was already late for my meeting but decided caution was more important, so I circled around my destination and then came back up Beethoven Strasse, where I was once again walking against the traffic. I found the sign for Hind Esquire on a black placard on the left side of the road. I walked right in and was met by a receptionist sitting up high behind a massive wooden desk.

"Hi, I'm Pat Walsh; I'm here to see Mr. Hind." The heavy blonde middle-aged woman seemed put out by my presence. She picked up the phone and had a short conversation in German and then, after more than one disapproving glance, got up and led me through one of the three doors located behind her to an inner office. Mr. Hind was an older man, and based on the tissues on his desk and his nasal-sounding voice, he appeared to be suffering from a cold.

"I have been assured the shipment is in transit and that title has transferred. As I have already received payment from the buyer, I have deposited the balance owed to your account. That leaves only one final matter, Mr. Walsh." He stood up and with his cane, led me back into the reception area and then through another door that took us into a storage room. It was a clean and tidy storage room with good lighting. Various statues, vases, and artworks were neatly arranged in rows. Most were in boxes and protective wrapping, but some were not. Mr. Hind took me down an aisle and we stopped in front of *Samantabhadra* which was positioned against the far wall, opposite the door. The Buddhist statue was much bigger than I expected it to be. It was striking.

"What's this?" I said, pointing to a big rectangular object wrapped in paper. Mr. Hind began peeling the paper away.

"This is the base the statue will stand on. As you can see, it's been inscribed as you have directed. The base is made of stone; it's a fine Italian marble."

"Is it made of solid stone?"

"No, that would be too heavy; it's hollow inside. It's a marble box—even hollow it weighs half a ton."

"This is very nice. Thank you for finding this for me."

"It was no trouble."

"Why don't you take a few moments to review it. I'm running late. I'm afraid I have a phone call scheduled that I must take. I'll be back with you in twenty or thirty minutes."

"Sure, that's fine," I said.

I removed the rest of the packaging paper from the base. It was polished white marble that matched perfectly the white porcelain statue it would support. On the front was a small painted portrait of Cheryl. She was smiling and it was a beautiful picture of her. Inscribed next to her portrait were the words, "In loving memory, Cheryl Li 'Shu Xue Wong'" and the dates of her birth and death. Underneath it read, "She died a free woman."

I sat on a box across from the statue and the base and tried to picture it on the grass next to the Cathedral in Palawan. I decided it would be a very good memorial for Cheryl. I heard a scraping noise behind me, and, out of reflex, I raised my right arm in front of my face just as a garrote was looping around my head. The wire bit into my arm and I felt the pounding of a man's knee driving into the small of my back. From my seated position, I stood straight up and lifted the shorter man off of his feet. He held onto the garrote with both hands while I repeatedly drove my left elbow into his ribs. I couldn't shake him loose. The garrote was cutting deeper into my forearm. I stepped backward, then bent forward to shake him. Out of desperation, I leaped backward as if to do a back flip. I landed flat on my back, with the man underneath. I banged away at his face with the back of my head. The garrote loosened and I swiveled my body around to strike him. He was fast and strong. He let go of the garrote and delivered a flurry of punches into my face. I pushed him down by the neck and sat up straight. I straddled the man and then using my height and reach advantage, I began raining down a series of punches of my own.

The man was exceptionally agile. He bridged his back and bucked me off of him and then he sprang to his feet. The feeling was returned to my right arm and I was beginning to feel like I was at full strength. My nose was bleeding. The man across from me was bloody from a cut on his cheek. I recognized the man. It was Huang, the Chinese agent who killed Cheryl. The man reached behind his waist and produced a knife in his right hand. I reached behind me, searching on the shelf for something I could use as a weapon and found nothing. He danced for only a second before he made his move. He lunged forward with his knife hand in a straight jab. I twisted away from the knife thrust allowing my jacket to take the brunt of the blade and then I punched the man in the throat as his momentum carried him forward. He let go of the knife that was piercing my left side. I hit the man with a side kick in the chest and pulled the knife from my lower abdomen. I dove on top of him as he was scrambling to his feet. As I made contact, I swung the knife hard in an uppercut thrust and felt the knife bury deep into his abdomen. He started to double over when I stood him up straight with a knee to the face. I pulled the knife out of his body and stared into his black eyes. What I saw was more menace than pain. I held the man up by the throat with my left hand and the knife with my right.

"You made a big mistake shooting Cheryl," I said before I stabbed the knife into his brain through his left eye.

My heavy jacket had taken most of the knife blade, but I was still bleeding pretty good. I found some packing tape and bandaged the wound with a strip of my shirt and the tape as best I could. At least it contained the bleeding. Mr. Hind was going to be back any minute and I didn't want him to see the body. I looked around for a place to hide it.

I lifted the heavy stone top off the base. It weighed over two hundred and fifty pounds and I almost dropped it putting it down. I found a box of plastic trash bags and put them around the Chinese agent and then taped them closed. I folded the Chinese agent and dumped him into the stone box. I lifted the heavy marble lid back up onto the base and made sure it was properly seated. Then I went to find the storage area washroom. My nose stopped bleeding and the blood in my side was under control. When I returned to the storage area, I found out how the Chinese agent got in; the loading dock door was ajar. I closed the door and cleaned up as well as I could and then walked out of the storage area and into reception.

"Please tell Mr. Hind that everything is to my satisfaction. I'm afraid I can't wait; it seems both of us are behind schedule today."

The woman behind the reception desk nodded and went back to her computer screen.

I walked back to my hotel and called Mike.

"I've been stabbed, and I need some medical attention," I said.

"Where are you?"

"In Zurich. I'm at the Park Hyatt."

"Someone will come to you. How did you get stabbed?"

"Remember that Chinese guy who killed Cheryl? The one we captured?"

"Yeah."

"Well, I was checking on Cheryl's memorial and the guy attacked me."

"What happened to him.?"

"He died. The Chinese have been following me all morning. They must have a kill order on me."

"Are the police involved?"

"No, I don't think they'll become involved. I don't think the body will ever be discovered."

"Give me your room number and stay where you are.

I'll get a doctor to stitch you up and then we'll get you out of there. It might be a good idea to hide for a while."

"I know just the place."

"Let me guess. Siargao."

"Yup. If you need me, you'll know where to find me."

"Don't kill yourself surfing."

"Compared to working for you, surfing Cloud 9 is a walk in the park."

CHAPTER 28

PAPHOS, CYPRUS

I WATCHED THE US Government Gulfstream G550 taxi toward me. I was standing in front of the open hangar door of our Trident facility in Paphos. I had flown in only a couple of hours earlier. Mike had called me at the beach and insisted on a meeting. I couldn't persuade him to come to Siargao and he couldn't get me to travel to DC. We decided to split the difference and meet in Cyprus. He got the better end of the deal, but I had to give him an easy victory every now and again or he would think I was always taking advantage of him.

I greeted him at the bottom of the stairs.

"Do you want to talk on the plane or in the building?"

"Let's go into the Clearwater office; it's a secure area and you can stretch your legs."

Mike was hobbling pretty badly when we started toward the open hangar. It always took him a while to get going after sitting for a long time. I've known Mike for quite a while. We first met in the Army as platoon leaders in the Second Ranger Battalion. Years later, he hurt his leg falling into a ravine while we were both attending Delta tryouts. That was after Panama and the First Gulf War and before a litany of conflicts too long to name. It was several hundred yards through the hangar and into the Clearwater wing. Halfway through the hangar, Mike's limp was much less noticeable.

"How's the new job? Are you still going 24/7?" I asked.

"It's more travel, but I have better control over my schedule than I used to."

"I'm sure the wife's happy about that."

"Yeah, she is. She says hello, by the way."

"We need to get together sometime. Maybe the next time I'm in the Bahamas."

"She could use a vacation. We'll come down and meet you."

"If you ever want to use the house, even when I'm not around, just let me know."

"Thanks, I might take you up on that someday."

We made our way to the conference room and I fixed both of us a cup of coffee.

"Why all the urgency? Do we have another mission for us?"

"No, that's why I needed to see you in person. I want to update you and see if you can help us resolve a few things."

"Ok, update away."

"A truce has been called on the tit for tat between us and the Chinese."

"Why? I thought we were winning."

"People were getting killed on both sides. We got all we wanted when we kicked them out of the Spratlys; after that, we were just inflicting pain to help bring them to the bargaining table."

"What's wrong with just continuing to inflict pain?"

"We've been running the risk of starting a hot war, for one thing. We were losing good people and we were starting to take some serious heat from some of our allies like the Greeks."

"Oh, that."

"Yeah, that."

"No more spitball fighting with the Chinese. It's a shame because only last night I thought of a really cool way to shut down the Panama Canal."

"Your creativity in creating mayhem is underappreciated."

"I've always thought so. The masters are seldom recognized while they're still alive."

"Ending the hostilities. That's the first point I wanted to cover."

"What's the second?"

"In every truce, there's a prisoner swap. One of the names the Chinese are asking for back is our friend Huang."

"That's the guy that killed Cheryl. I told you already, he died trying to kill me."

"We need to produce him, or at least a body."

"You can't just tell them he's dead?"

"No, they won't believe us; they'll think we're holding him for interrogation."

"What's so bad about that?"

"It could end the truce. Just tell me where the body is and we'll do the rest."

"That might be a problem."

"Did you destroy the body?"

"No, I had to hide it fast and the only place I could find was the stone base on Cheryl's memorial."

"You buried Huang in Cheryl's memorial?"

"That's what I said."

"Where's the memorial?"

"On the Cathedral Grounds of Puerta Princesa, Palawan."

"Jesus, that's disturbing. What were you thinking?"

"Honestly, I was just looking for the fastest, most practical way to hide the body. But after that, I kind of liked the idea. It has a Shakespearean quality to it, don't you think?"

"More like Poe and no, I don't like it at all. Some people would say it has a ritual murder quality to it, which is something neither the Chinese nor the organization I work for is going to think is a good thing."

"The only murderer is Huang. He shot an unarmed woman in the head. I killed the little bastard with his own knife. I was unarmed on an errand to pay my respects to Cheryl. That's not murder— that's self-defense. And I think it's only fitting that he spends eternity ass up in a stone box with a Buddhist god and his elephant sitting on top of him."

"That's troubling. I may have to get you another psych eval."

"Fine, but bring back the Schneeberger girl, enough with the old women."

"That's Doctor Schneeberger."

"That's the one. Let's get back to the point. Huang was part of a team. I took out a Chinese tail before I encountered him. They should have figured out he was killed; they should've been covering his back. Why are they asking for him now?"

"There are a lot of question marks about what happened

in Zurich. The Chinese had a team following you from the time you left Paphos. But I don't think Huang was part of that team. I think he went maverick to take you out. The Chinese don't do subtle. If they had an official kill order on you instead of a surveillance order it would have been like the Bahamas with lots of foot soldiers and not just Huang and one guy tailing you."

"It felt like killing me was personal to him."

"I think you wanted him dead. This was personal for you. So personal that every time you visit Cheryl's memorial, you'll be reminded of exacting your revenge."

"That's pretty deep. Are you reading pop psychology books?"

"Pop psychology? What I'm trying to get through to you is that this isn't in the realm of pop, this is deep in abnormal psychology territory."

"People don't kill murderers and mount them under the memorials of their victims anymore? Is that what you are saying?"

"We might have to recover Huang's remains and return them to the Chinese. Let's move on to the third point."

"What's that?"

"Sorenson's replacement. Your team needs a fifth man."

"Huang killed Sorenson too. Yet another reason for him to suffer in the afterlife."

"I sent you some files. I need you to interview the candidates and make a decision. We can't hold onto these guys forever—they have other options."

"Ok, I'll stay around here for a few days and take care of it."

"Then are you going back to Siargao?"

"No, I think I'll take the *Nomad* back to the Bahamas."

"That's a good place for you. You may want to talk to your friend Father Tellez about sticking Huang heels up under Cheryl's memorial." Mike got up and we walked back to his airplane. I watched him limp up the stairs. He was in a good mood; even from the side, I could see he was smiling. I think I amuse Mike. Plus, the craziness of these past months was behind him and I'm guessing that any respite is something to be savored in his business.

CHAPTER 29

BEIJING, CHINA

THE MINISTER OF State Security sat behind Huang's desk. Lined up in front of him were the senior officers from Huang's Task Force. Despite the suits and ties, all four men were standing at a rigid position of attention.

"What do you men have to say for yourselves?" the Minister said in a loud voice. The oldest, most senior member of the group, Colonel Lu, was the only one who dared to speak.

"Sir, we've completed our search for Brigadier Huang. We're convinced he's dead."

"Where is the body if he's dead?"

"Sir, we have extensively reviewed security camera coverage from the Zurich storefronts. Many of the buildings had good camera coverage including the antique dealer's business, Hind Esquire. The video coverage clearly shows Pat Walsh entering the building from the front and Huang entering the building from the loading dock in the rear."

"And how does that prove conclusively that Huang is dead and not captured by the Americans?"

"Pat Walsh is captured on video exiting the building. He leaves alone and departs on foot. He appears injured when he leaves. Huang is not seen leaving the building. All of the exits are covered by cameras. We have questioned the receptionist and the owner; neither saw Huang inside the building."

"What does any of this mean?"

"We believe Pat Walsh killed Huang and hid the body. We think the body was disposed of in a way that the owner was not aware of it—in the garbage, perhaps."

"What makes you think the CIA didn't pick up Huang from the building?"

"Because the only activities to and from the building were trash removal, deliveries, and shipments. None of the businesses involved had any relationship with the CIA. We tracked down the people and businesses associated with every license plate that stopped near the building for days after Huang was there."

"The disappearance of Huang remains an unsolved mystery.

"Yes, but we are confident he is dead."

"Why did Pat Walsh visit the business?"

"He was buying an 18th Century Buddha statue."

"What for?"

"It was a memorial for his girlfriend, Cheryl Li, the Chinese Intelligence agent Huang killed in the Bahamas."

"Really?"

"Yes."

"Where is the statue now?"

"We tracked it to a Catholic Cathedral in Palawan, Philippines. Here, we had a photo taken of the statue on display on the Cathedral grounds."

The Colonel handed the minister an 8 x 10 photo of *A Dehua Seated Figure of Samantabhadra* sitting atop a small grassy hill with the spires of a Catholic cathedral in the background. The Minister studied the photo and took notice of the image of Cheryl Li on the base of the statue along with her Chinese birth name.

"I will keep this photo," he said.

"Of course," the Colonel replied.

"We will officially classify Huang as dead, and the investigation of his death is now closed." The minister got up from the desk and left the office with the picture in hand. He took the elevator up to his office and sat behind his desk. He thought for a minute and a grin broke out across his thin grey features. He pulled out a pad of stationery from his center drawer and wrote a short note to the PLA Commander.

"I thought you might want to know that MSS has located your agent, Colonel Shu Xue Wong. May her demise give you comfort as you journey into your well-earned retirement."

The Minister smiled as he attached the note to the photo and slipped the two documents into an envelope. He buzzed his secretary.

"Have this delivered to the PLA Commander," he ordered.

The forced retirement of the PLA Commander was a source of great joy for the Minister. Losing the Spratlys was a mistake not to be forgiven by the President. The Minister daydreamed of being the hero who took them back. The Chinese forcibly occupied the islands in 2010 after the American President signaled that he wouldn't come to the defense of his Asian allies. Eventually, another like-minded individual would inhabit the White House; it was a democracy, after all, with the inevitable ebb and flow of ideas and convictions.

The Minister sat back in his chair with his hands behind his head. It was regrettable, what became of Huang; he served him well and played a key role in vanquishing his rival and in elevating his status with the President. Ping was President for life, but he was twenty years older than the Minister and had not chosen a successor. The new social credit score system managed by MSS gave the Minister great power to stymie any upcoming rivals who would get in the way of his true ambition, which was to follow in the footsteps of President Ping. The South China Sea affair was a huge opportunity that he made the best of. He felt greatly satisfied with his performance.

CHAPTER 30

PAPHOS, CYPRUS

THE FOUR OF us were seated around the table in the Clearwater conference room. We'd been reviewing CVs and military records for the past two hours. Mike supplied us three candidates to choose from and we were deadlocked over two of them.

"Does anybody know these guys personally?" I asked.

"I know both of them," Savage replied.

"And you prefer Ramirez over Tully?"

"Yes."

"Why?"

"They're both competent operators. I wouldn't object to either, but if given the choice, I think Ramirez is the better fit for this group."

"What do you know about a fit for this group? You haven't been here long enough for us to know for certain if you're even a fit."

"What do you mean by that?" Savage asked.

"You barely speak. I was about to enroll in a sign

language course to communicate with you; I thought you had a disability."

"How can anyone get a word in with you around? That's why I want Chi Chi Rodriguez. He's the only guy I know who can keep pace with your motor mouth," Savage said.

"Chi Chi Rodriguez. Wasn't he a PGA golfer back in the seventies or eighties?" I asked.

"Chi Chi is his nickname. You'll like this guy; he was pretty famous within the unit for his practical jokes."

"Since when are practical jokes a selection criterion?" Migos asked.

"What is it you don't like about the guy?" I asked Migos.

"He's a squid for one thing."

"McDonald's a squid. You get along well with him."

"McDonald isn't an Alpha Squid. He was on the teams, but he was a medic."

"You object to Rodriguez because he was an Alpha Squid. That's it, seriously?"

"Yeah. He'll be writing books and blogging about every one of our missions and we'll probably have to hire a cameraman and a public relations team. That's what squids do."

"Rodriguez did his Tier 1 time with CAG and if Mike forwarded him to us, he's already passed a CIA polygraph where they would have asked about that kind of stuff. What's your next objection?"

Migos sat quietly with his arms folded in front of him.

"If everything else is even, then it comes down to personality and compatibility," McDonald said.

"This isn't E-Harmony.com—this is a military operation. I don't care if Chi Chi completes you, Savage. I say we go with Tully," Migos said.

I laughed. I knew Migos didn't care who got picked; he was just trying to score points and annoy Savage.

"What do you say, Pat? You're the chairman of this committee. In the event of a tie, you vote twice. You've already voted for Tully once," Migos said.

"I'm good with Rodriguez."

"Why'd you flip?"

"He's going to be Savage's battle buddy; his vote is what counts. I'm happy with either one and it might be good to have another person on the team besides McDonald who knows what he's doing in the water," I said.

"Clearly favoritism; I'm going to HR," Migos said.

"All right, let's hold one more vote and make this official. Everyone for Rodriguez, raise your hand," I said.

All four hands went up.

"Chi Chi Rodriguez it is, then," Migos said.

"Savage, you can contact him and onboard him with the team."

"No problem."

"I think we should do a team bonding exercise to speed up fitting him in with the group," Savage said.

"What do you have in mind?" I asked.

"A surfing trip," Savage said.

"Now you're sucking up to the boss. You went from Helen Keller mute to a groveling kiss ass in a minute. What's gotten into you?"

"Rodriguez and I are very good surfers."

"You surf? I said.

"I grew up in Hawaii; of course I surf."

"Why didn't you ever mention that before?"

"I don't know; you never asked."

"Anybody else around here surf?"

"Muy Muy Migos has never surfed, but how hard can it be if Savage can do it? Color me in."

"What about you, McDonald?" I asked.

"I was stationed in Hawaii once, but I never learned. I'll bandage you guys up after you damage the coral."

"I was going to head back to the Bahamas, but a week in Siargao with you guys might be fun. I know a great place to stay and I have a daily routine already worked out that I'm sure you'll love. I'll handle the logistics. Get Chi Chi Rodriguez on a plane heading West," I said.

AUTHOR NOTES

Dear Reader, I hope you enjoyed Rising Sea. I would really appreciate a review on Amazon if you are so inclined. As with all of my books, in Rising Sea there's a lot of overlap between fact and fiction. I took more than a few liberties with the science around creating a man-made tsunami. I have no idea if such a thing is actually possible. Tests were done on the concept in New Zealand after the second world war, but the experiments never generated anything as big as what's described in the book. The other weapons and tactics used in the book are real and the descriptions are accurate to the best of my knowledge. Lady Chang and the Red Flags really were a scourge in 19th Century China, and they were defeated by the Portuguese and Chinese in the battle of the Tigers Mouth. Lady Chang did come to the rescue of her husband and negotiate a surrender to the Emperor, but as far as I know there was never any pirate treasure involved. The disputed Chinese occupation and construction of military bases on the Spratly Islands is a well-known fact.

As you may have noticed, I like travel, and I like to eat. A lot of what I write about is places I visit and things I like to do. Occasionally, I write about a place or an experience before I've ever visited. For example, I've never been to Siargao. I have a trip scheduled very soon and I plan to surf Cloud 9. I'm hoping it doesn't kill me. If you have any ideas, questions or comments about my books, feel free to write me at jlawrence@tgg-us.com

   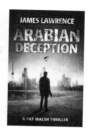

Links to James Lawrence's other adventure thrillers:

Be among the first to learn about future releases of Pat Walsh's adventures, just click the link below.
SIGN ME UP

TURN THE PAGE FOR A STUNNING PREVIEW OF
ARABIAN VENGEANCE

THE MOST POPULAR PAT WALSH ADVENTURE

CHAPTER 1

BRUSSELS, BELGIUM

AHMED ELEIWI ZIPPED his leather jacket against the wind as he exited the Bruxelles Central Train Station and entered downtown Brussels. It was a Saturday afternoon and the station was crowded with visitors on their way to enjoy a sunny spring afternoon shopping and sightseeing in the Grand Place Square. As he passed through the main doors of the station, he drew a second look from one of the soldiers positioned in the entryway. Belgium's response to the reoccurring terrorist incidents over the past year had been to station hundreds of military personnel throughout the city. In the congested downtown Brussels area, it was becoming increasingly difficult for a man Middle Eastern in appearance to travel unmolested. Ahmed was purposely carrying no bags to avoid arousing too much suspicion. Despite his efforts, the soldier signaled for him to come over and gave him a quick pat-down from top to bottom. Ahmed reminded himself that it was just a random search and forced himself to remain calm.

Despite his heart kicking into high gear, Ahmed slowly

walked away from the guard and continued at a leisurely pace past the Hilton Grand Place Hotel and through the arch passageway, taking him into the square proper. As he entered the Grand Place, Ahmed stopped to get his bearings. Along one side of the rectangular cobblestone square, a rock band was playing on a stage set up against a building wall, midway along one of the sides. It was early afternoon, and the UNESCO World Heritage site was crowded with a festival atmosphere. Tourist guides hustled to corral their charges across the expanse to the many historical and architectural items of interest. It was Earth Day, and several hundred protestors, still wearing green shirts and carrying signs from the morning march, congregated near the stage. The protestors were drinking beer, dancing to the music and having a great time in the unseasonably cool weather.

The small square was bordered by four- and five-story gothic buildings made of grey stone and adorned with gold accents, archways and magnificent spires. He searched for the City Hall, with its distinctive nighty-six-meter tower holding the Archangel Michael. Having found his bearings, he confirmed he was in the northeast corner.

Ahmed looked west and found the Hard Rock Café sign only fifty meters from his location. He checked his cell phone and found a text: "3rd Floor, window." Ahmed stepped inside the narrow restaurant entryway and walked through the souvenir shop to the hostess. Before she could offer to help him, Ahmed interrupted and volunteered that his wife was on the third floor, waiting for him. The hostess pointed him to the stairs. Slightly winded from the climb up the steep spiral staircase, Ahmed emerged from the stairs and surveyed the crowded third-floor dining room for

Raghad. He spotted his Iraqi contact in the last table along the windows. He walked directly to her, gave her a peck on the cheek and slid into the seat across the table. Raghad acknowledged Ahmed and turned her attention back to the baby she was feeding in the high chair to her left.

Forcing a smile, Ahmed reached across the table and placed an affectionate hand on the baby's head in greeting. The waiter came over, and although Ahmed had no appetite, he ordered a hamburger and a liter of Leffe Blonde Beer. The window seat had an excellent view of the entire square. Ahmed estimated the crowd at over six hundred in the confined twenty thousand square feet of space. His pulse was racing, and he began to sweat. His beer arrived, and he gulped it down and ordered a second potent Belgian Beer. When his glass was empty, he nodded to Raghad and reached down under the table to retrieve a heavy diaper bag. He struggled sliding the heavy bag across the wooden floor.

Leaving it concealed under the table, Ahmed opened the bag. His practiced hands found the safe to arm switch by feel, and he moved it forward into the arm position. Pulling the bag out from under the table, he slid out of the booth and walked away from Raghad and her baby with the heavy diaper bag on his shoulder.

Ahmed could feel Raghad's eyes bearing down on him as he emerged from the restaurant and navigated his way through the heavy crowd toward the stage. He expected Raghad would wait until he was near the stage, where the densest cluster of people could be found, before triggering the explosive device. He could tell from people's reactions that they were starting to notice the growing panic that was reflected on his face. No longer able to feign calm, Ahmed began to hurry, crashing into people as he scurried toward the stage.

With her baby in her arms and a remote control designed to look like a baby toy in her hand, Raghad watched Ahmed through a window. Seeing Ahmed's panic, she ducked behind a nearby support pillar and triggered the device. Twenty meters from the stage, all six daisy-chained claymore mines, arrayed in a horseshoe inside the diaper bag, exploded. Each claymore, containing one and a half pounds of C4 explosive, launched seven hundred steel balls into the crowd with lethal force. In seconds, every person in the tiny square went from vertical to horizontal. The concussive force trapped inside the square shattered the windows of the Hard Rock Café and all of the surrounding buildings.

Raghad reappeared from the protection of the pillar to witness the devastation. The flying glass had lacerated the exposed and thinly covered skin of the people sitting closest to the windows. Screams and cries for help filled the restaurant.

Worst hit were the Earth Day protestors who had been gathered around the stage moments before. The activists inadvertently served as human shields as they absorbed the brunt of the lethal projectiles before they could reach the larger crowd. A Chinese tourist group was killed in its entirety when the focused spray from a single claymore hit them head-on while they were lining up for a picture.

The damage done by the blast was grotesque. In the first fifty meters fanning out from the stage, few of the bodies remained intact. It was a macabre sight of blood and dismembered bodies. When the last fatality was recorded nine days after the attack, the death toll would reach 174, with another 269 wounded.

CHAPTER 2

NEW YORK CITY

MICHAEL GENOVESE FELT the familiar burning in his lungs as he once again ratcheted up the pace. His target was less than a hundred yards in front of him, running with a steady, even gait that was deceptively fast.

Michael ran the same six-mile Central Park loop every day. At thirty-eight, he kept himself at the same peak level of fitness he had enjoyed while playing point guard on the basketball team at Harvard. The man he was chasing had passed him two miles back, and now his only goal in life was to retake the lead before his route ended.

His narrowing vision registered the Strawberry Fields marker off to his left, meaning he had less than a mile left to make his move. Michael took great pride in never having allowed anyone to beat him on his daily run. The pain intensified as he nudged the pace. With only a quarter mile to the finish point, he pushed it even harder. His legs were on fire, and there was a searing pain in his lungs. He could feel his vision narrow further as he forced his breathing and pumped his oxygen-deprived legs.

When he closed to within twenty yards of the interloper, he noticed it was a younger man in his twenties. The runner was oblivious to Michael as he effortlessly glided along the course, listening to music through his earbuds. Michael's breath grew even more ragged, and he was saturated in sweat as he transitioned into a full sprint for the last hundred meters to the imaginary finish line.

Barely passing the runner in the last few feet before reaching the end of the course, Michael slowed to a walk and ducked off the trail before falling to his knees. It was a full ten minutes before he was recovered enough to stand and make his way back to his apartment. Tired, but euphoric from his victory, a triumphant Michael gingerly walked across the street and made his way into the private elevator that delivered him to his penthouse apartment.

The elevator opened into a large open foyer. When the doors slid open, the first thing that met his eye was Katrina, sitting on a bench along the side of the entryway. Her bottom lip was swollen and red, and she had a large purple welt on her left cheek. Surprised to see Michael, the skittish Ukrainian withdrew from the foyer and moved behind a couch in the living room. Michael ignored the willowy young blonde and stepped around her two suitcases on his way through the living room to the hallway that led to his bedroom. He made a mental note to contact his personal assistant and request a replacement.

Despite his money and good looks, Michael's penchant for rough play with the ladies had earned him a certain notoriety within his social circles. An unfortunate dating incident with a fiercely resistant actress who happened to maintain an enormous social media network had made him radioactive to the local ladies. That event had spurred him to get creative and discover a website that advertised itself as matching "sugar babies" with "sugar daddies." Michael found that for a nominal fee, he could import some of the most beautiful and willing creatures in the world directly to his doorstep.

When he'd started to find the constant internet searching and endless chatting and messaging needed to ensnare the prospective sugar babies to be time consuming and tedious, he'd pioneered a way to outsource the work. He'd expanded on the information age mail-order concept by hiring a virtual personal assistant from India.

Shahab's daily responsibilities included uploading and managing Michael's profile on several relevant websites. His virtual PA also had the use of a shared WhatsApp messaging account and a shared email account to line up girls for delivery on demand. Michael considered his unique outsourcing method of acquiring mail-order girls to be a textbook case study in optimizing efficiencies through offshoring. Once he'd gotten his system going, he found he had created a pipeline of beautiful girls who not only bolstered his image at social events, but also accommodated his carnal needs. It was pure genius.

On his way to the shower, Michael caught his reflection in the mirror array inside the master bathroom and had to stop. He removed his clothes and posed in different positions as he flexed his well-defined muscles. With the classic Italian good looks of a young Tony Bennett, Michael never tired of studying his reflection. His rigid diet and exercise regimen were rewarded with a single-digit body fat percentage. His six-pack abdominals were his pride and joy and the focus of his gaze. As he flexed with his hands clasped in front of him in what bodybuilders referred to as the crab pose, he thought back to last night with Katrina and he swelled with pride.

After showering, Michael drove to Long Island to have lunch with his brothers. The family home was a twenty-two-thousand-square-foot estate that had been built by his father in 1969. His grandfather, Vito Genovese, had been the Don of the Genovese Crime Family until his arrest in 1957. With roots tracing back to Lucky Luciano in the 1930s, the Genovese family was sometimes referred to as the Ivy League Mafia.

After Benny "Squint" Lombardo had taken the reins following Michael's grandfather's death in prison, Michael's father, Salvatore, had used his sizable inheritance to concentrate on enterprises other than the family staples of loan sharking, drugs, gambling, prostitution and protection. At the beginning of the Vietnam War, a prescient Salvatore Genovese had invested in defense companies. He'd sent his three sons, Gino, Michael and Louis, to the best prep schools and the best colleges. Gino had attended Fordham, Michael, the scholar-athlete, had studied at Harvard, and Louis had gone to Columbia. After graduating from college, the three sons had worked with their dad and, by the mid-1990s they had assembled a strong portfolio of minority positions within the defense industry.

After Salvatore had succumbed to cancer in 1999, the three brothers had worked to secure majority shareholding positions and to unify their defense portfolio under a single management team. G3 Defense had been founded in 1999, and by 2017, the company had revenues exceeding seventeen billion dollars, twenty-seven thousand employees, and sixteen fully owned subsidiaries. In only eighteen years, G3 had become one of the largest defense firms in the United States.

Despite being the middle son, Michael was the chairman and CEO. Gino served as CFO, and Louis was the COO. The board of directors included the three brothers plus the external financiers, which included two private equity firms and Nicky Terranova, the second cousin of Barney Bellomo, the current head of the Genovese mob.

The family estate was Gino's birthright as the oldest son. He and his wife graciously hosted the extended family gathering every Sunday. Gino and Louis were both married and had five young children between them. Michael, the bachelor was a favorite uncle and despite his birth order a patriarchal figure within the family.

Michael parked his Mercedes behind Louis's Range Rover in the driveway. He was barely out of the car before being swarmed by three of his nephews, Louis, Joey, and Danny. The boys moved as a pack, attempting to submit their uncle, imitating moves learned from televised wrestling and UFC MMA. After fifteen minutes of roughhousing, he declared a draw and the joyful boys allowed a disheveled and grass-stained Michael to continue on his way to the main house.

He was met at the door by Gino's wife, Stephanie, who greeted him with a hug.

"Why do you encourage them, Michael? They ruined your good shirt."

"I don't care about the shirt. It's how boys play, Steph," said Michael.

"One of these days, they're going to hurt you."

"I think I have a few years left when I can handle them," said Michael as Stephanie led him into the kitchen by the arm.

After dinner, the three brothers retired to the home theater to watch the Yankees play the Orioles. The brothers were seated in leather recliners, drinking beer in front of an eighty-inch plasma TV and waiting for the start of the game.

"Have you been following the news about what's going on in Belgium?" Michael asked.

"Yes, that was terrible. Those Europeans need to get serious about those immigrants," said Gino.

"I bet we see a spike in our Security and Detection revenues. Nobody sells body scanners better than those jihadis," Louis said.

"That's not the only good that'll come of it. That guy from Abu Dhabi isn't going to be a problem anymore," Michael said.

"What guy in Abu Dhabi? What are you talking about, Michael?" said Gino.

"Nothing… just that I heard a rumor about that guy who was digging into our business a while back. Seems he might have some bigger things to worry about," Michael said. Gino and Louis looked at each other with puzzled expressions and then switched the subject back to the NBA Playoffs.

CHAPTER 3

ELEUTHERA, BAHAMAS

P AT STRADDLED HIS surfboard and positioned himself so that he could watch the incoming swells over his right shoulder and see the beach over his left shoulder. It was a sunny spring day. The rolling waves were turquoise until they broke into a white foam and raced onto the blushing pink strip of sand.

Beyond the beach, Pat could see the top floors of his beach house peeking above the gently swaying palms. He shifted his gaze downward and surveyed the surf line, looking for Diane. He spotted her in a sea of white, working her way out through the surf. Every seven seconds she would vanish under an incoming wave and then reappear without missing a stroke. She moved fast, with the grace and power of an elite athlete. Diane smiled as she reached Pat. It was a dazzling smile accompanied by emerald-green eyes set in a stunningly beautiful face.

"Are you a tourist or a surfer?" asked Diane.

"I'm enjoying the view while I wait for the perfect wave."

"The tide's starting to go out, and it's only going to get worse. You better take what you can get."

"Yeah, you're right. One last wave, then it's time for lunch."

Pat and Diane carried their surfboards under opposite arms as they walked to the house. Between the beach and the house was a narrow trail encroached by lush ground vegetation. The two threaded their way through the narrow trail, past the guesthouse and the pool house until they reached the main house, a three-story peach-colored stone mansion with eight bedrooms.

Pat had been staying at the beach house for almost five months, and the daily surfing and regular workout routine had him in better shape than he had been in a long time. The beach house was his retirement dream home, everything in it built to his specifications. The second-floor deck was his favorite spot, offering a view of the Atlantic Ocean to the east and the Caribbean to the west.

Diane was a surfer girl from Florida. The two had met a year ago when she was waitressing at Tippy's, the neighboring beachfront restaurant where he was a regular customer. Over a period of months, the relationship had progressed from customer and waitress to surf student and surfing guru, and then to soulmates. Pat was head over heels in love with Diane, and for the past three months, the two had lived a honeymoon existence at the beach house.

Pat was just stepping out of the shower when he received a call from Jessica, his office manager. The Trident headquarters were located three miles up island in Governor's Harbour. Trident was a CIA subcontractor that had a single contract with the US government to supply military goods to US allied forces in Syria and Iraq.

Pat answered the call, and before he could even say hello, a panicked Jessica interrupted.

"We have a serious problem."

"What's going on?"

"All of our bank accounts have been frozen, and our export license requests, purchase orders and payments have been put on hold by the government contract office," said Jessica.

"Any idea why?"

"They didn't even give me notice. I was trying to transfer money from the CITI account online and it rejected every transaction. I tried the same with the accounts in the Bahamas and got the same thing. Then I received a notice from DCMA that our contract is suspended, still with no explanation."

"Give me a few minutes to make some calls, and I'll get back to you," said Pat.

Using the secure app on his CIA-issued smartphone, Pat called Mike Guthrie, a friend from his days as a junior officer in the Second Ranger Battalion. The two had gone their separate ways after Delta selection and had been reunited seventeen years later in Afghanistan, when Mike was a CIA agent and Pat was a down-on-his-luck defense contractor working as a military advisor to the Afghan National Army. Mike had recruited Pat as an asset, and the two had been working together professionally for last five years. Mike was currently assigned to Langley in the Clandestine Operations Directorate, while Pat's company, Trident, was part of a black operation that was managed by the Department of Defense. Trident was the conduit for military supplies to the Peshmerga and other forces fighting against ISIS in Syria and Iraq.

When, after ten rings, Mike did not pick up, Pat terminated the call. He looked across the table to Dianne. "I don't have time to explain this. Just pack a bag. We need to be out of here in five minutes."

Pat stood from his chair at the kitchen table and sprinted up the stairs toward his office on the third floor. He quickly opened his safe and removed two packages. One held passports for both him and Diane, and the second contained cash and cell phone SIM cards. Next, he went into a storage closet and withdrew a duffle bag. With the bag filled, he ran downstairs and entered the garage through the kitchen entrance, throwing the heavy black nylon duffel bag into the back of the Tahoe. Diane entered the garage a few seconds later, and they both jumped into the Tahoe and sped off.

Less than a mile away, on the Caribbean side of the island, was a small marina that was home to a small local fishing fleet. The sole recreational vehicle in the marina was Pat's sixty-four-foot motor yacht. The Azimut 64 Flybridge had been his home for three years when he'd lived in Abu Dhabi, United Arab Emirates. Since his relocation to the Bahamas, beyond the occasional fishing trip or quick day trip to Nassau, the boat had largely been ignored.

Pat detached the external power connection and untied the boat from the slip while Diane went to the wheelhouse and started the twin Caterpillar 1150-horsepower engines. Runway Cove Marina had a very narrow access point designed for the smaller fishing vessels. Navigating the narrow passage and the sharp dogleg turn was a tricky maneuver that would have been impossible without the bow thrusters. Once through the gap and into the Caribbean, Pat gradually increased the speed to twenty-eight knots and set a heading for Nassau, fifty miles to the west.

Diane approached Pat while he was sitting at the helm station on the flybridge.

"What's going on?" asked Diane.

"Honestly, honey, I have no idea. All I know is that the US government has suspended my IDIQ contract, and all of my business and personal bank accounts have been frozen," said Pat.

"Are you in trouble with the IRS or something?" said Diane.

"You've seen the scars on my body, and you have a general idea of what I used to do for a living. The government contracts Trident supports are so sensitive I'm not even allowed to discuss them, but they're essential to US policy, and they aren't something that can be casually suspended without serious cause," said Pat.

"So, what does that mean?" said Diane.

"It means anything big enough to cause the government to shut down my business operations is serious enough to make me want to disappear until I can get ahold of the people I work for and figure out what the hell is going on," said Pat.

"Are we in danger?"

"I don't think so. When the US government freezes your bank accounts and cuts off a contract that's strategically important, it must mean an arrest is soon to follow.

The only reason I didn't leave you at the house is that I don't know who's after me."

"Why would the US government arrest you?" said Diane.

"I haven't done anything wrong that I know of, but having my money and my business contracts frozen and my contact in the CIA unavailable has me spooked," said Pat.

"Now I'm scared."

"Throw your phone overboard. We need to remain unfindable until I can figure this thing out," said Pat.

It took almost two hours to sail to Nassau Harbor. Diane was clingy for most of the trip, and while Pat would have preferred to spend the time planning, instead he'd found himself responding to an endless stream of questions and concerns from Diane. During the few respites from her desire to be assured, he'd quietly debated whether it would be safer to drop Diane off in Nassau. Ultimately, he'd decided to keep her with him. Partly out of selfishness, since he couldn't stand to be away from her, and partly because he knew it would cause her just as much pain for her to be away from him. It was poor operational reasoning, and he hoped he wouldn't regret it.

Pat docked at a transient slip in the Palm Cay Marina. Unlike his tiny fishing marina in Governor's Harbour, the Palm Cay was built for luxury tourism, and with one hundred and ninety-five mostly occupied slips, his yacht blended in perfectly. Pat booked for two days and paid the docking fee of two dollars per foot per day to the harbormaster. Once they had the power and water connected, they locked up the boat and walked to the car rental office located inside the marina clubhouse.

"What's next?" asked Diane.

"We need to provision the boat with food for a three-week journey. There's a Fresh Market a few miles from here that should have everything we need. We also need lunch, and I need to find Wi-Fi so I can contact my people. Once we load up and prep the boat, we'll fill the external fuel tanks. That'll give us a range of close to three thousand miles and then we'll be ready to depart tomorrow morning," said Pat.

"Depart for where?"

"At this point, it's more about getting off the grid. I really don't have any particular destination in mind."

"That doesn't sound like much of a plan," Diane said with a smile. Pat put his arm around Diane and kissed the top of her head.

"It's not, but if it turns out I have to be on the run, we might as well make a holiday of it."

The first stop was lunch. Still unwilling to put a cell phone in operation, Pat used the navigation system on the rental car and settled on a nearby restaurant called Luciano of Chicago. It was almost three in the afternoon, and the restaurant was nearly empty. While he was waiting for his shrimp and scallop ceviche appetizer, Pat turned on his laptop and connected to the restaurant's free Wi-Fi. Using a TOR app, he was able to mask his IP address and location and encrypt his communications. He went on Google Messenger and sent a message to Mike Guthrie.

"The contract has been suspended and all my personal and business accounts are frozen. What gives?" he wrote.

After devouring a magnificent seven-ounce filet mignon with asparagus and mashed potatoes, he received a reply from Mike.

"Explosives used in Brussels bombing originated from Trident. JTTF has identified you as a subject of the investigation, and an arrest order has been issued," Mike replied.

"Does the JTTF know what I do and who I work for?" wrote Pat.

"No. The director wants to avoid a scandal. The case against you is strong and getting stronger. Disappear and give me some time to find out who's pulling the strings on this," Mike replied.

"Done, will check back with you daily on this channel."

"Any updates you want to share?" Diane asked. Pat sipped his double espresso while looking across the table at Diane's concerned expression.

"The good news is that there's no physical danger. The bad news is as I suspected. I need to disappear while the people I work for clear this problem up."

"What do you mean by disappear?"

"It means we spend a few weeks on the Atlantic, looking for the perfect wave," Pat said.

Diane smiled. "Being on the run with you sounds like fun."

Made in the USA
San Bernardino, CA
24 May 2020